SELBY SUPERSNOOP

DUNCAN BALL
ILLUSTRATED BY ALLAN STOMANN

Angus&Robertson
An imprint of HarperCollins*Publishers*

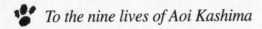 *To the nine lives of Aoi Kashima*

The author would like to thank Josie Walker, Fleur Hall, and Kathryn Lambert for invaluable (and therefore, unpaid) assistance cheerfully rendered.

Angus&Robertson
An imprint of HarperCollins*Publishers*, Australia

First published in Australia in 1995
Reprinted in 1995

Text copyright © Duncan Ball 1995
Illustrations copyright © Allan Stomann 1995
Music copyright © Kathryn Lambert 1995

HarperCollins*Publishers*
25 Ryde Road, Pymble, Sydney, NSW 2073, Australia
31 View Road, Glenfield, Auckland 10, New Zealand
77-85 Fulham Palace Road, London W6 8JB, United Kingdom
Hazelton Lanes, 55 Avenue Road, Suite 2900, Toronto, Ontario M5R 3L2
and 1995 Markham Road, Scarborough, Ontario M1B 5M8, Canada
10 East 53rd Street, New York NY 10032, USA

National Library of Australia Cataloguing-in-Publication data:

Ball, Duncan, 1941–   .
  Selby supersnoop.

  ISBN 0 207 18565 4.
  1. Dogs – Juvenile fiction. I. Stomann, Allan.
  II. Title.
A823.3

Printed in Australia by Griffin Paperbacks, Adelaide

10 9 8 7 6 5 4 3 2
99 98 97 96 95

CONTENTS

BEFOREWORD

The adventures in this book are all
absolutely true. They aren't eggs...
ecs... exx... exaggerated one little
bit. Some of them are about me
learning to be a detective.
I called it SELBY SUPERSNOOP
because detectives snoop
around and some people call
them snoops. I know you
think I'm bragging by putting
in the SUPER part and maybe
I am super (just a little).
You'd be a super detective
too if people thought you were
just a harmless dog and
you were really Selby, the only
talking dog in Australia and
perhaps the World.

Selby 🐾

SELBY SUPERSNOOP, DOG DETECTIVE

Selby was all alone and bored silly. There was nothing on TV and no good books to read. Or were there?

Selby climbed to the top shelves of the bookcase in the study to see if there were any books he hadn't read. Just when he was about to climb down again, he spied a dusty old book. It was *The Art of the Private Investigator* by Mary Touchstone, P.I.

'Very interesting,' Selby thought as he flicked the book off the shelf with his paw and let it crash to the floor. 'I've always wanted to be a detective.'

In a second, Selby was curled up on the lounge reading the back cover. As he read, his jaw began to quiver with excitement.

Thrill to the mystery, romance and adventure of the world of the private investigator! Amaze your friends! Have your enemies arrested! Earn big money in crime detection and have a great time! Don't waste another minute. Read this book and your life will be changed forever!

'Mystery, romance and adventure, wow!' Selby squealed. 'That really makes a medium-sized dog's spine tingle. I can't wait to have my life changed forever!'

With trembling paws, Selby opened the book and began to read:

Anyone can become a private investigator, or a P.I. as we are known. So settle back, follow this easy step-by-step guide and soon you will be solving mysteries all over your neighbourhood.

'I'm settled back, Mary,' Selby said out loud, 'and ready to solve mysteries all over my neighbourhood. I can't wait!'

All afternoon Selby read through chapters called 'How to be a Master of Disguise', 'How to Spot a Criminal', 'How to Tail a Suspect', 'How to Find Clues', 'How to Overpower People' and 'How to Eavesdrop'. It was all there: everything Selby had always wanted to know about solving crimes and catching criminals.

Finally Selby read the last paragraph in the book:

Just remember that the world of the private investigator is the world of mystery. Nothing is the way it seems. Look for clues everywhere and suspect everyone and you can't go wrong. Happy detecting!

'What a great book!' Selby cried. 'But where am I going to find my first case? Bogusville is such a boring place. There's never any crime or anything.'

But Selby had spoken too soon. The very next day, just when Selby was wondering how he could use his new detective knowledge, there came a knock at the Trifles' door.

'Excuse me, Dr Trifle,' the woman said, 'my name is Eve Amery.'

'The toy soldier collector,' Dr Trifle said, snapping his fingers. 'I saw something about you in the newspaper years ago. Come right in.'

'They're *model* soldiers. They're not really toys.'

'How may I help you?'

'There's been a crime committed and I need your help.'

Selby's head shot out from behind the lounge.

'A crime!' he thought. 'An actual real live crime here in Bogusville!'

'What crime?' Dr Trifle asked.

'Someone is stealing my model soldiers,' Eve said. 'Let me explain. Emery—he's my brother—and I live in a house across town. The soldiers were our grandfather's and when our parents died, they became ours.'

'They're fighting a battle, I believe.'

'Yes, in a big glass case with hills and trees and trenches. Recently Emery and I decided to sell them but suddenly they started disappearing.'

'Disappearing?' Dr Trifle said.

'Disappearing,' Selby thought.

'Someone is stealing them,' Eve said. 'Every Tuesday some go missing. Every week there are fewer and fewer. There are practically none left.'

'Have you been to the police?' Dr Trifle asked.

'Yes, and they were very helpful. But they don't

4

think anyone is breaking in. We have locks on our doors and bars on all the windows, you see.'

'Then what's happening?'

'I'm ashamed to say that the police think that Emery—my own dear brother—is taking the soldiers, Dr Trifle.'

'But why would he steal what he already owns?'

'No, no, *we* own them. The police think he's selling them and keeping all the money for himself. Every Tuesday evening he catches the bus to the city to visit friends, you see. He could be taking the soldiers then.'

'Why don't the police arrest him?'

'Because they have no proof.'

'I see,' Dr Trifle said. 'So you think that because I'm an inventor I might have an invention that could tell if your brother is taking the soldiers?'

'Do you?' she asked with a smile.

'Possibly. May I see one of these soldiers?'

Eve Amery handed three soldiers to Dr Trifle who studied them carefully.

'Got it!' he said. 'Each soldier has a hole down the middle. We could slip a little specially charged magnetic strip in there where no one will see it. Then we hide my Super-Sensitive Magnetic Screaming Theft Detector in the bushes outside your house. If anyone walks by with a soldier then—'

Dr Trifle let out a loud, wailing, machine-like scream. Eve Amery and Selby covered their ears till he stopped.

'That's marvellous,' Eve said. 'May I see this Super-Sensitive Magnetic Screaming Theft Detector of yours, Dr Trifle?'

'Yes, of course. As soon as I've made one. I just thought it up a minute ago. But don't worry; I'll have one ready by Tuesday.'

That night Selby lay awake listening as Dr Trifle worked on his new invention.

'This is great!' Selby thought. 'Now all we have to do is spring the trap and catch Eve's brother in the act! Hey, that almost rhymes!'

On Tuesday evening, Dr Trifle and Sergeant Short hid in the bushes as Eve Amery said goodbye to her brother. None of them knew that Selby had sneaked across town and was hiding in a tree nearby.

'This is so exciting!' he thought. 'I'm a real snoop now!'

Just then, Emery walked down the path and the lights, horns and bells in Dr Trifle's Super-Sensitive Magnetic Screaming Theft Detector flashed and honked and tinkled all at once.

'What's that noise?' Emery screamed.

'I'm afraid you're under arrest,' Sergeant Short said, stepping out of the bushes.

'For what?'

'For stealing model soldiers and taking them to the city to sell.'

'You've got to be kidding,' Emery said. 'I don't give two hoots for those stupid things. I wouldn't be caught dead with one!'

By now, Dr Trifle was pointing a second invention, his new Miniature Hand-Held Super-Sensitive Magnetic Pinging Theft Detector, at Emery's left-hand coat pocket and it was going *ping ping ping* so fast that it sounded like the international ping pong play-offs.

'What's in that pocket?' Sergeant Short asked.

'Nothing,' Emery said, reaching in and pulling out five soldiers. 'Hey! How'd they get in there? This is a set-up! You put them in there!'

'I'm afraid you'll have to come with us,' the policeman said.

Selby watched as Dr Trifle and the policeman led Emery Amery away.

'Poor Eve,' Selby thought, sniffing a little sniff. 'She *thought* her brother was taking the soldiers but *knowing* is different. She must be grief-stricken.'

Selby was about to climb down from the tree when something in *The Art of the Private Investigator* came back to him.

'"Nothing is the way it seems",' he quoted. '"Suspect everyone and you can't go wrong".'

'Hey now, hold the show!' Selby thought. 'What if Emery isn't guilty? What if someone— his sister, for example—put the soldiers in his pocket?'

From where Selby sat he could just barely see in the window of the house. There was music playing and suddenly Eve Amery danced by, leaping and letting out a series of whooooopeeeees!

'If this woman's grief-stricken, then I'm a bandicoot's bottom!' Selby thought. 'Something very strange is going on around here.'

The music stopped and Selby saw Eve Amery dash to the telephone.

'I'd love to hear what she's saying,' Selby

thought, as he remembered the chapter of the book on how to eavesdrop. 'If only I could get into the house and listen in. If I can get from this branch to the roof maybe I could pull up a bit of roofing and climb in,' Selby thought, remembering the chapter called 'How Burglars Burgle'.

Quietly as a cat, Selby lowered himself onto the roof, pulled up a bit of roofing and climbed into the house. Through the ceiling he could hear Eve talking on the telephone in the room below.

'. . . no more problems now that my stupid brother is out of the way. I'll be on a plane and out of the country as soon as he's in jail. They're all mine to sell now! All mine! He'll never catch up to me!'

'Mary Touchstone, P.I., was right,' Selby thought as he crawled towards a crack in the ceiling to see down. 'But how will I tell the police that Eve framed her brother?'

Selby moved forward again and felt something jab his paw.

'Ouch!' he cried in plain English. 'That hurt!'

There was dead silence below. Selby squinted in the darkness and saw that he'd stepped on a little model soldier. Around him

in the darkness he now saw dozens more.

'So this is where she hid them!' Selby thought.

Suddenly Eve, hearing Selby's cry, stood on a chair and opened the secret trapdoor in the ceiling, all of which would have been okay if Selby hadn't been standing on it at the time. In a second, the door swung down and Selby dropped straight onto the woman, knocking her to the floor unconscious.

'Now to ring the police,' Selby said, getting up and shaking off a dozen model soldiers.

In a second, he was speaking to Sergeant Short.

'I have some important information about the Amery case,' Selby said, putting on a deep detective-like voice. 'Emery is innocent.'

'Really?'

'Yes, really. His sister, Eve, planted those soldiers on him. She hid the others in the ceiling of their house. She was going to sell them and keep all the money for herself.'

'Who are you?' Sergeant Short asked.

'Never mind who I am,' Selby said. 'Just get over to the Amerys' house straight away and you'll find Eve asleep on the floor.'

'We're on our way,' the policeman said. 'But tell us how you found all this out.'

'I listened in to a telephone conversation she was having,' Selby said. 'That's what tipped me off.'

'You were listening in? You mean you eavesdropped?'

'You can bet your boots I did,' Selby laughed. 'You should have seen me—I dropped right on top of Eve!'

SELBY IN SUSPENSE

'Talk to me, you dummy dodo dog!' Willy demanded. 'You talk to me! I know you can talk so you'd better do it now!'

Selby was dangling upside down, suspended by a rope tied around his foot. Willy pointed his new video camera at Selby's face.

'You talk to me or else!' Willy said. 'Then I'm going to show the video to everyone. They'll know I'm not lying.'

Selby sighed a dog-like sigh and rolled his eyes.

'The brat must think I'm a complete idiot,' Selby thought. 'There's no way I'm ever going to talk to him again no matter what he does to me. I'll just dangle here from his stupid booby trap till the Trifles find out what's happening. Then Willy will be in big, big trouble. How did I ever get myself into this mess?'

Getting into the mess had been easy: Selby knew that Aunt Jetty was going to leave her dreadful son, Willy, with the Trifles while she went shopping. But Selby was on the lookout and ready to hide at a moment's notice. As soon as they pulled up in front of the house, he was going to head for his favourite hiding bush in the backyard. Willy would never find him there.

That was the plan—but then Dr Trifle came out of his workroom with another brilliant new invention.

'I call it Breath-Away Miracle Window

13

Cleaner,' Dr Trifle said, proudly holding the spray bottle next to the front window.

'Window cleaner has already been invented,' Mrs Trifle pointed out.

'Yes, but I hate all that rubbing and scrubbing. There are always streaks when you finish and you can never get into the corners. Breath-Away is different—watch,' Dr Trifle said, spraying the inside of the front window.

'It's gone all cloudy and white,' Mrs Trifle said. 'I can't see a thing.'

'Just stand back and watch.'

Sure enough, soon the window cleared and was cleaner than Selby had ever seen it before.

'That's brilliant!' Mrs Trifle said. 'But where did the dirt go?'

'It fell down onto the windowsill,' Dr Trifle explained. 'Now all you have to do is blow it away. That's why I call it Breath-Away. I also called it that because it's such a brilliant invention that it takes your breath away.'

'I'm not sure about this blowing the dirt away business,' Mrs Trifle said, wiping the specks of dirt from the windowsill with a rag. 'But it certainly does work. How about going outside and cleaning the other side of the window?'

Selby stayed inside the house and saw the doctor suddenly disappear as he sprayed the window.

'He's so clever,' Selby thought. 'I wish I was good at inventing inventions.'

Suddenly the glass cleared and there, standing next to Dr Trifle, was the hideous sight of Aunt Jetty.

'They're here!' Selby thought as he ran into the garage and then shot through the hole in the wall and into the backyard. 'I've got to get away before that crazy kid catches me.'

Just then there was a *sproing!* and a *whizzang!* as Selby's foot landed right in Willy's booby trap. In a microsecond, Selby was pulled up into the air like a rocket.

'Got you this time!' Willy giggled, pointing his video camera at Selby. 'Now you talk, mister stink-face stupi-bottom dog! Talk right now!'

'No way,' Selby thought. 'Fat chance. Not on your life! You've got to be dreaming. This kid must think I'm a total idiot. I'll hang here till the cows come home but I'm never ever going to say a word.'

Selby could hear Dr Trifle talking to Aunt Jetty inside the house.

'Be nice to Willy,' Aunt Jetty was saying. 'The poor darling is feeling a bit sad ever since his goldfish died.'

'His goldfish died?' Dr Trifle said.

'Willy put him in the washing machine. He wanted to watch him surf. Apparently the little fellow wasn't much of a swimmer because he drowned or something.'

'Don't you worry about Willy,' Dr Trifle said as Aunt Jetty drove away. 'Hmmm, I wonder where he's got to?'

Just before Dr Trifle came around the corner of the garage, Willy pulled the release string on his booby trap and Selby came crashing to the ground.

'Oh, there you are, Willy,' Dr Trifle said. 'Having a little play with Selby, are you?'

'He doesn't like me,' Willy whined. 'Look! He just lies there like a dumb-head!'

'He's probably having a rest,' Dr Trifle said, spraying some Breath-Away Miracle Window Cleaner on the lens of Willy's video camera. 'Come and play with the computer.'

'Every bone in my body aches,' Selby thought as he limped to the back of the yard and curled up in his hiding bush. 'Some day, somehow I'm going to get that kid and when I do I'll . . .'

But before he could think of what he'd do to Willy, Selby fell sound asleep. He slept for a while and then something struck him—it was a big stick.

'Wake up, stupo,' Willy said, waving the stick in the air.

Selby jumped to his feet and without so much as a second thought, dived for the hole in the back of the garage. But just as he was flying through the air and thinking of how he was going to block the hole and lock Willy out, he remembered Willy's booby trap.

'Oh, no! It's probably right inside the garage!' Selby thought as he sailed through the air. 'I think he's tricked me again!'

Sure enough, just as Selby's head went through the hole he saw the loop of Willy's rope lying on the floor. But Selby tucked his legs up tight like a broad-jumper trying to jump an extra centimetre, and glided over the rope and onto the floor beyond.

Just then, Willy came scrambling through the hole—right onto the rope.

'Yike!' Willy yelled as the booby trap caught

his leg and flung him up to the ceiling. 'It's got me!'

The sight of the tiny torturer swinging from a rope was too much for Selby. He let out a long, un–dog–like laugh.

'It's not funny,' Willy whimpered.

'If you could see how silly you look,' Selby said in plain English, 'you'd laugh too.'

'You talked! You talked!'

'Of course I talked,' Selby sighed. 'You know perfectly well I can talk. But it won't do you a bit of good because nobody believes a word you say.'

'I'm telling!'

'Tell all you want.'

Just then, Dr and Mrs Trifle opened the door to the garage and found Willy dangling from the rope.

'I do believe you've been caught in your own trap, Willy,' Mrs Trifle said, untying the rope and lowering him down.

'That dog talked to me!' Willy screamed.

'Come, come now, Willy,' Dr Trifle said. 'You're old enough to know that dogs can't talk.'

'He can and he did,' Willy said, running for a shelf and picking up his video camera. 'And it's on my video! It was going all the time! Put it in the TV! You'll see!'

'Oh, no,' Selby thought. 'The kid tricked me. He wasn't trying to catch me with the booby trap. He was trying to catch me on his video camera—and he did! I've been outwitted by a half-wit nitwit!'

'I'm sure you're wrong,' Mrs Trifle said to Willy.

'You look!' Willy cried. 'Look at the video!'

'All right,' Dr Trifle said, taking the tape out of Willy's hand. 'If it'll make you happy.'

Selby followed the Trifles into the lounge room. Dr Trifle wound the video tape back a bit and then pushed the PLAY button.

'Oh, no!' Selby thought. 'This is it. I'm gone. They'll have to believe Willy now. I can't stand it! I can't let that little brat tattle on me. I'd rather tell them myself.'

Selby stepped up next to the Trifles and cleared his throat. He was about to say, 'Excuse me, but I'm afraid that Willy is right—I *can* talk,' when the video began playing.

The first thing Selby heard was his own voice saying, 'If you could see how silly you look, you'd laugh too.'

'That's him talking!' Willy screamed, pointing at the TV. 'That's Selby! He talks! See?'

'I don't see anything,' Mrs Trifle said. 'I can hear a strange voice but I can't *see* anything. Are you sure that voice isn't from a TV show?'

'No, no, it's him! It's that dummy dog!'

Selby looked over at the TV, which was all white and snowy. Dr Trifle fast-forwarded the tape and then fast-backwarded it, but it was no use—there was no picture.

'That's very odd,' Mrs Trifle said, suddenly looking over at the window which Dr Trifle had used to test his miracle window cleaner. 'And look, this is even odder: that window cleaner has made the window go all white. You can't see through it anymore.'

Selby looked at the window and then at the lens on Willy's video camera. It, too, had gone white.

'Oops,' Dr Trifle said. 'I think that window cleaner isn't such a miracle, after all. And I think I've ruined Willy's camera.'

By now Mrs Trifle had fast–backwarded the tape to the beginning—the part before Dr Trifle's lens cleaning, when Selby was hanging upside down by his leg.

'Willy!' she cried. 'You horrible child! No

wonder Selby doesn't like to play with you! Look what you did to him! I'm going to give you a good, hard spanking for being so cruel to Selby!'

'No, don't spank me!' Willy cried as the first blows began to fall on his bottom. 'My goldfish died and you have to be nice to me! Mum said you have to! Ooooooooowwwwww!'

'Well, I don't know,' Selby thought as he headed for the backyard again. 'I guess some things do turn out all right after all. That Breath-Away stuff turned out to be a miracle for me. And it certainly is taking Willy's breath away right now!'

SELBY ON THE LOO(SE)

Selby was a very lucky dog. Well at least he thought he was lucky. That is, he would have been lucky if it hadn't been for a sudden streak of very bad luck just when everything was going so well.

It all happened the day that Dr and Mrs Trifle were going to dinner at Mascara Mansion. The mansion was the huge old house that the fortune-teller, and now cosmetics millionaire, Madame Mascara, had just bought.

'She's so proud of that house,' Mrs Trifle said. 'She's invited the most important people in Bogusville to dinner—and us, too.'

'What do you mean, *and us, too*? We're important, aren't we? Why, you're the mayor of Bogusville,' Dr Trifle said.

'I guess I just don't think of us as being

important,' Mrs Trifle said. 'We're just little old Trifle us. We certainly don't live in a forty-two room mansion.'

'Especially not one that's haunted,' Dr Trifle said with a wink.

'I forgot,' Mrs Trifle laughed. 'She really believes there are gremlins living there, doesn't she?'

'I'm afraid that Madame M believes in all those supernatural things: ghosts, goblins, gremlins, ghouls—and that's just the ones starting with G. That's why she bought the house.'

'You forgot genies and gnomes.'

'Are you sure they start with G?' asked Dr Trifle who wasn't a great speller.

'Pretty sure. Anyway, gnomes or no gnomes, we're invited to dinner and Phil Philpot who runs The Spicy Onion Restaurant is going to do the cooking. It should be a lovely evening.'

'Oh, I'd love to live in a huge mansion,' Selby thought as he listened to the Trifles' conversation. 'I'd have hundreds of servants and TVs in every room and my own private movie theatre. Oh, how I'd love to go to Mascara Mansion tonight and have some of Phil Philpot's wonderful peanut prawns! Just my luck: the Trifles will leave me here with a bowl of those awful Dry–Mouth Dog Biscuits. Oh well, at least I'll have a chance to play some games on the computer.'

'I thought maybe we'd take Selby along with us tonight,' Mrs Trifle said.

Selby's ears shot up like rockets.

'Are you sure that Madame M won't mind?' Dr Trifle asked.

'No, no. She loves Selby ever since she told his fortune ages ago, remember? She specifically said we could bring him along.'

'I can't believe it!' Selby thought. 'They're actually going to take me with them! I can't wait! Oh, lucky me! Peanut prawns, here I come!'

Selby's luck began to change the moment he entered the gates of Mascara Mansion.

'Oh, you've brought the little poochy-poo,' Madame Mascara cooed. 'Isn't he a darling little doggy-woggy?'

'Forget the poochy-poo and the darling doggy-woggies,' Selby thought as he trotted into the mansion after the Trifles. 'Take me to the tucker; I'm one hungry hound.'

All the guests were seated in their finest clothes around the great, long dinner table.

Everywhere there was the sound of sizzling food and the heavenly smell of peanut prawns.

'I've made a special dish for Selby,' Madame Mascara said, putting a bowl of Dry–Mouth Dog Biscuits on the floor. 'Otherwise he'd have to eat people-food and I know he'd hate that!'

'Oh, woe. I should have known it was too good to be true,' Selby thought as he crawled under the table and chewed a dog biscuit. 'I wish they'd left me at home.'

Throughout the meal everyone listened politely as Madame Mascara talked about all the ghosts and gremlins she'd heard in the house.

'Oh, bother,' Selby thought. 'I've got to go to the loo. How will I ever get out of this place?'

Selby went down the hallway and up to the huge oak front door where he barked a couple of barks.

'They'll never hear me,' he thought. 'Besides, this is silly. Why should I have to go out in the cold when I could use a perfectly good people-loo?'

Selby looked down the hallway.

'If I'm quick about it, no one will notice.'

Selby dashed off down the hall and then had one last look at the dinner guests before turning the corner and ducking into the loo. He quietly closed the door and in a second was finished, flushed and ready to return to the dining room.

'I feel like a real person,' he giggled. 'That was fun!'

Selby went to open the door and realised that the knob was so high that he couldn't reach it, even standing on his hind legs.

'Uh-oh,' he thought. 'I'm going to have to figure out some way of getting up there. Hmmm. Don't panic. Don't panic. Don't panic.'

Selby scanned the room for anything to climb up on.

'I know!' he said, opening a cupboard and pulling out a dozen rolls of toilet paper. 'I'll make a poo paper pyramid.'

Selby made a pile of toilet paper rolls and climbed on top of them. He reached up slowly, stretching his paw towards the knob. At any minute he expected the rolls to fall out from under him and he'd go tumbling down.

His paw felt its way up, higher and higher, till he touched cold metal.

'That's it!' he thought. 'I've got it!'

Just then, there was a sudden, loud knock at the door.

'Is anyone in there?' a woman's voice boomed.

Selby quickly pushed the big brass bolt across, locking the door.

Then there was another knock followed by another.

Selby froze.

'What now?' Selby thought, trying even harder not to panic. 'I'm trapped like a rat! Oh, woe, woe.'

'Will you be long?' the voice asked. 'I'm in rather a hurry.'

'I'll stay quiet till she goes away,' Selby thought.

But just as he thought this, the toilet paper rolls slipped out from under him and Selby went crashing to the floor.

'Are you all right in there?' the woman yelled. 'Hey! Somebody, help! I think someone's collapsed in the loo!'

'Oh, no!' Selby thought. 'Now they're going to batter down the door. I've got to think of something, fast!'

Selby's mind went in every direction at once like a flock of lost racing pigeons.

'I'm all right,' Selby said finally, putting on a high voice. 'I'll just be a minute.'

'I beg your pardon?'

'I said, I'll just be a minute.'

'Are you sure you're okay?'

'Yes, of course I'm okay. Just go away.'

'I'll wait right here, if you don't mind.'

Selby felt himself getting angry. Why couldn't she just go away and leave him to escape?

'Couldn't you find another loo?' Selby asked.

'This is the only one.'

'But that's ridiculous. There must be dozens in this dump.'

'Listen here, I happen to own this dump. I'm Madame Mascara. And who might you be?'

'None of your business,' Selby said. 'Just go away and leave me in peace.'

'Don't tell me what to do. I'm going to stand right here till you come out!'

'Crumbs,' Selby thought. 'I've got to think of another way out of this place, fast!'

Selby looked around the room. There were no windows and no skylight; only a fan in the wall.

'If I can pull the fan out of there, maybe I could climb through the hole,' he thought.

Selby leapt up on the toilet, forgetting that the lid was still up, and landed right in the cold water.

'Oh, great. Now I've really put myself in it.'

Selby jumped out and closed the lid. In a minute he'd pulled the fan out and watched it go crashing and sparking to the floor.

'What's going on in there?!' Madame Mascara screamed. 'What do you think you're doing?'

'Everything's okay,' Selby said. 'I'm just having a little difficulty here.'

'And I'm going to break this door down.'

The full weight of Madame Mascara slammed against the door. When it didn't open, she tried again and again.

Then, just as the screws holding the lock

began to pull out, Selby leapt for the hole in the wall. His head and front legs shot through to the outside but, unfortunately, his middle didn't quite make it.

'I'm stuck!' Selby thought. 'And Madame Mascara is about to come face to face with a talking dog! Well, not exactly face to face . . . Oh, why didn't I just go to the loo in the bushes like a normal dog?!'

Then, just as the slamming reached its peak, Selby took a deep breath and pushed against the outside wall, popping himself through the hole and tumbling to the ground.

Inside there was the splinter of wood and the cry, 'Where are you? Where'd you go?!'

Selby caught a glimpse of Madame Mascara's black hair poking through the now opened hole as he tore around the corner of the house and in through the front door. Inside he could see all the dinner guests running down the hall towards the loo. By the time they returned to the table, Selby was lying innocently under the table finishing off a plate of Phil Philpot's finest peanut prawns.

'I swear there was someone in there,' Madame Mascara laughed. 'But there couldn't have been. No one could have got through that hole.'

'You mean, no *person*,' Mrs Trifle said.

'Oh, I see what you mean,' Madame Mascara said. 'It must have been one of those gremlins I told you about. You see; I knew the mansion was haunted.'

Later, as the guests were leaving, Madame Mascara leant down and patted Selby on the head.

'Such a lovely dog,' she said. 'I hope he enjoyed his dog biscuits.'

'I'm sure he did,' Dr Trifle said, wondering why there was peanut butter on Selby's breath.

'Well, toodle-oo, poochy-poo. I hope you had a good time. You're such a quiet little doggy-woggy.'

'Toodle-oo, my paw,' Selby thought as he trotted off with the Trifles. 'That was my big mistake—this poochy-poo should never have gone *to the loo*.'

THE FURRED FRENZY

'Look at this little kitten!' Mrs Trifle said as she came in patting the ball of fur she was cradling in her arms. 'Isn't he absolutely gorgeous?'

Selby lay on the floor watching Dr Trifle paint a picture of some scenery.

'A k-kitten?' Dr Trifle stammered. 'You didn't buy him, did you?'

'No, he belongs to Postie Paterson. He asked me to look after him for a few hours. Postie said to think of a name for the little sweetie.'

Mrs Trifle put the kitten down on the carpet. The kitten snuggled up to Selby and then fell sound asleep.

'Isn't he a darling?' Selby thought. 'Kittens are so cute. I wish the Trifles would get one. I'd have so much fun.'

'I suggested the name *Sunny* because he has

such a warm and sunny nature,' Mrs Trifle explained. 'But Postie said he couldn't use it because it's the name of the rhino at the zoo. He said that every time he hears it he thinks of five hundred kilograms of dangerous, horn-headed beast.'

'Fair enough. I guess we'll have to put our thinking caps on,' Dr Trifle said.

Mrs Trifle looked over at her husband's painting.

'For an inventor,' she said, 'you're not a bad painter. Such pretty mountains. What's it a painting of?'

'Bogusville, of course. It's a birthday present for my cousin.'

'Hmmm,' hmmmed Mrs Trifle. 'Exactly which part of Bogusville is it?'

'Just look out the window and you'll see.'

Mrs Trifle looked out the window and didn't see anything that looked at all like the scene in the painting, except for the tree in the backyard.

'I'm still a bit confused,' she said.

'About what?'

'Your painting is of a very up and down sort of place. It has rocky cliffs and mountain peaks and snow and glaciers and all that.'

'That's because my cousin only has a narrow place on the wall for the painting. He needs an up and down sort of painting to fit it.'

'But Bogusville is more a side to side sort of place,' Mrs Trifle said. 'You could even say that it's dead flat.'

'That's exactly why I've had to change it.'

'And you've put in lots of snow. The closest thing the people of Bogusville have seen to snow was when the Girl Guides camped in Bogusville Hall and had a giant pillow fight. By midnight the air was so full of feathers we thought it was a blizzard.'

'Ah, yes, I remember,' Dr Trifle said, dabbing some more snow on the mountain peaks. 'But none of that matters. My cousin has never been to Bogusville so he doesn't know that there's no snow or mountains.'

'Well, I'm sure he'll like it,' Mrs Trifle said. 'But there's something else about the painting that bothers me. I can't quite put my finger on what it is.'

'Yes, I know what you mean,' Dr Trifle said. 'There's something missing, isn't there?'

'It's obviously not mountains. You've got plenty of them.'

'You can always tell a good painting because it makes you feel all warm inside when you look at it,' Dr Trifle said. 'This one doesn't make me feel warm.'

'Perhaps it's all that snow,' Mrs Trifle said helpfully.

'No, no, I've got it! It needs a person in it,' Dr Trifle said. 'People give paintings warmth. A painting without people is like . . . like . . .'

'A sandwich without bread? A car without tyres? A dog without a bone?'

'Exactly,' Dr Trifle said, looking Mrs Trifle up and down the way painters do when they're going to paint a picture of you.

'I have an urgent errand to run,' Mrs Trifle said, remembering how he'd given her crossed eyes the last time he painted her. 'Why don't you put little fluffpuss here in the painting? That'll give it warmth.'

'Good idea!' Dr Trifle exclaimed, mixing up some kitten-coloured paint. 'I'll paint him right on the limb of that tree.'

Mrs Trifle dashed off and Selby watched as Dr Trifle quickly painted the kitten into his picture. When he'd finished, the doctor stood back and looked at his work.

'The rest of the painting's okay,' Selby thought, 'but there seems to be something wrong with the kitten part.'

'The kitten's okay,' Dr Trifle said out loud, 'but there seems to be something wrong with the rest of the painting. It still doesn't give me a warm feeling. Maybe I'll mow the lawn and see what I think of it later.'

'You are a little cutie, my furry little purrer,' Selby said, rubbing his nose against the kitten's warm fur when the doctor had left the house. 'Maybe Postie will let you stay here with us.'

Suddenly Selby was aware of two little eyes staring back at him.

'You want to play, don't you?' Selby said and then, 'Yowch!'

In a flash, the kitten leapt up and dug its tiny claws into Selby's nose, raking them along until they stuck fast.

'Stop it!' Selby squealed, pulling the kitten's claws out of his nose.

Before Selby knew what was happening, the kitten ran up the side of the lounge, did a flip in the air and sank his tiny teeth into Selby's leg.

'Stop that, you tiny little terror!' Selby cried. 'It hurts!'

The kitten scampered round and round in circles in front of Selby, scratching at Selby's legs, head and tail as he went.

'I'm not playing with you—you're too rough!' Selby said. 'Your teeth and claws are like razors!'

The kitten looked at Selby for a minute, yawned and then curled up and went to sleep again.

'That's more like it. You're cute when you're asleep,' Selby thought, looking back to Dr Trifle's painting again and suddenly realising what was wrong with it. 'I know. Dr Trifle forgot to paint your whiskers! A kitten isn't a kitten without whiskers. I'll paint them in for him. A few little white lines and the painting will be perfect. Dr Trifle is so absent-minded that he'll think that he painted them.'

Selby squeezed some white paint onto a tiny brush and began delicately painting the whiskers on the kitten's face.

'That's great!' he said. 'I'm already getting that warm feeling that Dr Trifle was talking about.'

Selby was just painting in the last whisker when suddenly a small blob of fur flew through the air and landed smack on his painting paw.

'Now look what you've done!' Selby yelled, shaking the kitten off and looking at the wide white stripe that ran down the middle of the painting. 'You've ruined it! Uh-oh, the lawn-mower's stopped. Dr Trifle will be in here in a second! Oh, no! Here he comes. And here comes Mrs Trifle too!'

Selby put down the paintbrush and curled up on the carpet as Dr Trifle and Mrs Trifle came in and studied the painting.

'That's much better,' Mrs Trifle said. 'Now I think it has that warmth you wanted.'

'So it does,' Dr Trifle agreed. 'Your idea about putting in the kitten was a good one.'

'I don't think so. I think it's that big white ray of sunlight that made the difference.'

'The ray, yes, that ray gives it warmth,' Dr Trifle said, trying to remember when he'd painted it. 'Come to think of it, *Ray* would be a good name for the kitten.'

'Why yes!' Mrs Trifle said. 'It reminds me of *Sunny* because of a *ray* of sunlight. It's a warm and friendly name. It really suits the little dear. Postie will love it!'

'That kitten's about as warm and friendly as a chainsaw,' Selby thought as he licked his sore paw and glanced down at the kitten. 'What *Ray* reminds me of is those *ra*zor-sharp teeth and claws!'

SELBY BITES BACK

It was an innocent mistake.

Mrs Trifle's dreadful sister, Aunt Jetty, was staying at the Trifles' house—fortunately without her even more dreadful sons, Willy and Billy. Yes, it was true that Selby didn't like her. You could even say that he hated her. But he *never*—not in a million years—intended to bite her. Even if he *had* wanted to bite her, he certainly wouldn't have bitten her *on that part of her body!*

It all happened one day when Selby was secretly re-reading a part of *The Art of the Private Investigator* about how to use dogs to catch burglars. The book lay open on the floor of the study and Selby was curled up in the chair above it, pretending to sleep—but secretly reading through squinting eyes.

It was such an interesting chapter that Selby didn't see Aunt Jetty come into the room. Then, Aunt Jetty—not looking carefully and thinking that Selby was just a big fluffy pillow in the chair she was about to sit in—started to sit down.

In that last fraction of a second before the quivering bulk of Aunt Jetty's bottom came down on top of him, Selby suddenly realised that something was wrong and looked up. Selby's jaw dropped open and he froze in terror, but there was no time to move.

'Ooooooooooowwwwwwwwwww!' Aunt Jetty screamed, leaping to her feet again and rubbing her bottom. 'Come quickly! That savage dog has just bitten me on the posterior!'

'On the what?' asked Mrs Trifle, coming into the study.

'He chomped me,' Aunt Jetty exclaimed, 'on my hindmost part!'

'He did what to your what?'

'Don't you understand? He bit me on the old sit-down. On me bot-bot. On the back bumper bar, the dum-de-dum.'

'I still don't follow you.'

'Well that's exactly it—the part that follows me! Heavens, woman, he's just nipped me on

the part of me that's facing south when I'm travelling north.'

'Oh, you mean he bit you on the bum.'

'You don't have to be crude about it.'

'But he's never bitten anyone in his life—not on the posterior or the bot-bot or on anything,' Mrs Trifle said, patting Selby's head. 'I wonder what's got into him.'

'All I know is that my bottom is riddled with teeth marks and it hurts like blue blazes!'

'I'm terribly sorry,' Mrs Trifle said.

'And now I want you to ring the police,' Aunt Jetty said. 'I insist he be put down like any other ill-mannered menace.'

'Put down!' Mrs Trifle gasped, covering Selby's ears when she said it. 'Don't you ever use that sort of language in this house! It's just lucky that he can't understand you or his feelings would be mightily hurt. No one—nothing—in this house is going to be put down, do you hear?'

Selby was about to say, in plain English, 'Ahem, excuse me, but I'd like to tell my version of events: I was just lying there innocently reading when this great galumph mistook me for a cushion,' but he thought better of it.

'If you won't ring the police then I think I'll ring them myself,' Aunt Jetty said.

'You'd better think again,' Mrs Trifle said, 'because if you do, you will have to leave this house and never come back ever again!'

'Well,' Aunt Jetty said, thinking again, 'it's either that or I insist you take old what's-his-name to obedience classes to learn some proper doggy manners before he murders some poor helpless innocent person like myself.'

'I'll poor innocent her,' Selby thought as he wobbled his sore jaw back and forth. 'What a nerve! First she sits on me and then she wants to have me put down. She's the one who needs obedience classes!'

'What obedience classes?' Mrs Trifle asked her sister.

'This very afternoon, Sergeant Stiffjaw of the Federal Police Dog Squad is at Bogusville Reserve giving free dog obedience lessons. I suggest that you take this savage little beast there and see if it's possible to civilise him.'

'I'll think about it,' said Mrs Trifle, who wasn't about to be pushed around by her sister but who thought that a dog obedience lesson might be interesting to watch.

And so it was that Mrs Trifle took Selby to the park and found twenty other dog owners and their dogs watching as Sergeant Stiffjaw put his police dog, Biff, through his paces.

'Walk!' he screamed. 'Stop! Heel! Fetch! Sit! Shake hands!' and Biff did just what he said, and stood as stiff as a statue between commands.

'Biff has to be the dumbest dog I've ever seen,' thought Selby. 'Why does he take it?

Sergeant Stiffjaw has the poor thing acting like a robot. Who would want a robot for a pet?'

'If you decide to enrol your dog in my classes,' Sergeant Stiffjaw said, 'I'll also give them a special attack dog course as a bonus.'

'Goodness!' said Mrs Trifle. 'Why would anyone want to turn a loving pet into an attack dog?'

'Very simple,' said Sergeant Stiffjaw. 'To keep burglars from burgling. Even peaceful country towns like Bogusville have their burglars.'

'He's probably right there,' Selby thought.

'Let me give you a demonstration,' said Sergeant Stiffjaw. 'Okay, I'm going to be a burglar and you'll see what Biff does.'

Sergeant Stiffjaw buckled some padding to his arm and put a black ski-mask over his head. Already Biff was beginning to growl and bare his teeth.

'Okay, Biff,' he said, his eyes peering out through the mask. 'Attack!'

Biff barked ferociously and tore at his trainer with muscles rippling and fangs dripping saliva. He jumped into the air and knocked Sergeant Stiffjaw to the ground, growling and tearing at his sleeve. By now all the dogs except Selby were barking with excitement and pulling on their leads. Then the trainer took the hood off and yelled, 'Stop! Sit!' and Biff stopped immediately.

'Gosh! That was scary!' Selby thought. 'But there's no way *I'd* ever attack a real live burglar! A dog could get hurt!'

Selby's heart was still beating quickly from the attack demonstration when he noticed something moving next to a house at the side of the park. He could barely make out a dark figure creeping slowly through the bushes.

'A burglar!' he thought.

Selby saw Biff stiffen as he, too, noticed the hiding figure.

'He's about to break into that house!' Selby thought. 'If only I could tell Sergeant Stiffjaw; he'd have Biff attack him! But I can't tell him or I'll give away my secret! And I can't attack the guy myself because I'm just not an attacking sort of dog. Oh, no! What am I going to do? I think this is a case for some dog ventriloquism,' he added, putting a paw over his mouth.

No one was quite sure what happened next. It started with a mysterious voice yelling, 'Attack!'. Suddenly Biff was dashing towards the bushes followed by a pack of dogs. And in less than a second, Aunt Jetty—who had sneaked into the bushes to make sure that her sister had taken Selby to the obedience class—was scrambling up a tree with a dozen dogs tearing at her trousers.

'Jetty!' Mrs Trifle cried. 'What were you doing lurking in the bushes?'

'Call them off!' Aunt Jetty screamed as she dangled from a branch. 'This is all your fault! If that dead-head dog of yours hadn't savaged me, none of this would have happened!'

'Dead-head dog,' Selby thought as he smirked a secret little smirk and barely kept from giggling. 'Oh, bite your bum. Hey, what am I saying? That's how all this started in the first place.'

PEGLEG PEGGY'S TREASURE

'Look at this! An old map of an island!' Dr Trifle exclaimed.

Selby looked up from where he was lying to see Dr Trifle pull a piece of crumbly paper from the chair he was fixing.

'Are you sure, dear?' Mrs Trifle asked.

'Well, I know a map when I see one. Hmmm, where did we get this chair?'

'It's been in the family for years. It once belonged to my great, great, great, great, great, great-grandmother,' Mrs Trifle said, wondering if she'd said the right number of 'great's. 'Peggy Prescott was her name. She was an actor from Perth.'

'You don't mean Pegleg Peggy from Perth, do you?'

'Have you heard of her?'

'Yes, of course,' Dr Trifle said. 'Your great, great, great, great, great, great, whatever-she-was was very famous.'

'I have lots of famous ancestors,' Mrs Trifle said proudly.

'But she wasn't famous for being an actor,' Dr Trifle said. 'She was famous for being a pirate.'

'It's only a rumour.' Mrs Trifle blushed a little blush. 'There's no proof of it.'

'So maybe this map was hers,' Dr Trifle said.

Selby suddenly remembered the story he'd read about Pegleg Peggy, the pirate from Perth. She was such a terrible actor that finally they booed her off the stage and she went to sea and became a pirate. For years, she and her terrible crew of cut-throats looted ships all around the South Seas, stealing jewellery.

'They say she used to capture other actors,' Mrs Trifle explained. 'She'd take them back to her secret island and make them act in plays with her. Of course she always made herself the star.'

Dr Trifle and Mrs Trifle put the map on the floor and studied it as Selby secretly peered over their shoulders.

'I do believe it's a treasure map,' Dr Trifle said.

'Why do you say that?'

'Well, it has all these directions that say things like, "Turn right at the big rock and walk ten paces and then turn left". Besides, it says "Treasure Map" here in the corner.'

'So it does,' Mrs Trifle said. 'Do you suppose there's actual real live treasure buried on this island?'

'Well, you never know.'

'Treasure!' Selby thought as visions of trunks filled with jewellery flooded his brain. 'That would be great! We could be rich, rich, rich! Oh, how I'd love to be rich! How I love treasure!'

'The island doesn't have a name,' Dr Trifle said. 'It could be anywhere in the world. What good is a treasure map if you can't find the island in the first place?'

Suddenly Dr Trifle remembered the Island Finder programme in his computer. He dashed into the study and scanned the map into the computer. After a couple of *bings* and a *pip* and a *boop*, the answer came up on the screen.

'It's a tiny little island on the Barrier Reef called Traffic Island next to another island called Refuge Island,' he said. 'Traffic Island, hmmm. There are no roads or people on it, so how can there be traffic? Very strange.'

'I say we head for the Barrier Reef this weekend,' Mrs Trifle said, 'and do some digging. It'll be a good little adventure.'

The next day the Trifles caught a flight to an airport near the Barrier Reef. Selby was stuck in a tiny cage in the cargo section but, for once, he didn't mind.

'Rich, rich, rich! We're about to be filthy rich,' he squealed. 'I don't care if they've crammed me in this horrible box because soon they'll be buying me emerald-studded collars and gold and silver flea combs. I'll be the richest pet in the world! We'll live in a mansion with lots and lots of servants. *And finally I'll be able to tell the Trifles my secret!* It won't matter because they'll have so many servants that they won't have to put me to work! And I'll be able to sit in a normal aeroplane seat—a normal *first class* seat, of course.'

And so it was that the Trifles and Selby found themselves waiting on a pier at a place called Information Bay. In a few minutes a boat pulled in captained by none other than Captain Slick Slipway, the near-sighted former bus driver.

'Oh, not him again,' Selby thought. 'This guy is such a pain.'

'The bus is leaving in two minutes. Watch your step,' Captain Slipway said as the Trifles climbed on board the captain's very bus-like boat, the *Golden Doldrum*. 'Move to the rear, please.'

'We're going to Traffic Island,' Dr Trifle said. 'Do you know where it is?'

'Know where it is?' the captain cried, pulling the cord that went *ding ding* as he pulled away from the pier. 'When I gave up driving the number 275 bus and took to the sea, that sandy little blob didn't even *have* a name. I'm the one who named it Traffic Island. And I named the one next to it Refuge Island.'

'I thought it was a very bus driver kind of name,' Mrs Trifle said.

Two hours later, the *Golden Doldrum* was passing Traffic Island when Mrs Trifle suddenly cried, 'Hey! This is our stop.'

'You didn't ding the dinger,' the captain said as he pulled up to the beach. 'I'm not a mind-reader, you know.'

Selby and the Trifles scrambled ashore. By the time the boat disappeared into the distance, Dr and Mrs Trifle were standing next to the big rock and beginning to walk sixteen paces to the right, ten paces straight ahead, and then eight paces to the left.

'X marks the spot!' Mrs Trifle cried, plunging her shovel into the sand. 'Buried treasure, here we come!'

Selby sat back against a coconut palm having a daydream about buried treasure. In it Selby and the Trifles were dancing on the beach, throwing fistfuls of treasure into the air.

'Why do people always throw treasure up in the air instead of putting it in their pockets?' he wondered. 'They must get so excited they just can't help themselves.'

For the next hour Dr and Mrs Trifle dug the hole deeper and deeper and wider and wider and longer and longer, until it was big enough to bury the number 275 bus and the *Golden Doldrum*.

As the day wore on, Selby's visions of treasure began to disappear and he lay on the beach knowing that he'd now have to keep his secret forever.

'I give up,' Mrs Trifle said finally. 'I don't think there ever was any treasure. Let's go back to the mainland.'

'The bus—I mean, the boat—isn't due till

tomorrow morning,' Dr Trifle said, looking at the schedule. 'We'll have to camp here for the night.'

That night Selby curled up next to the campfire as the Trifles lay in their sleeping bags.

'Life is so cruel,' he thought. 'I was just about to be a free dog—a free *rich* dog—and now I never will be. Oh, woe woe woe.'

'I suspect that my great, great, great, great, great, great-grandmother wasn't a pirate after all,' Mrs Trifle said.

'It's true that actors are very impractical and unreliable people,' Dr Trifle said. 'They don't even know their left from their right. Pegleg Peggy might have even made up this whole treasure business.'

'He's right,' Selby thought. 'Actors don't know their left from their right.'

Selby remembered a play rehearsal he'd seen. Every time the director told the actors to turn to the right, they turned to the left. And every time the director said, 'Go left,' they went to the right.

Selby thought for a minute and then thought for another minute. By the time a third thinking minute came around, he'd jumped to his feet.

'But hold the show!' he thought. '*Stage* left

54

and *stage* right are just the opposite to *audience* left and *audience* right. When actors go to the left, they go to the audience's right. Maybe that's why Peggy's directions are wrong— they're all backwards!'

Selby waited until the Trifles were snoring quietly and then slipped the map out of the picnic basket along with a torch. In a second he was standing by the big rock.

'Let's see, now,' he said. 'First I take sixteen paces to the right—I mean to the left—then ten paces straight ahead, and then eight paces to the right.'

Selby stood on his hind legs and stretched out each step to make it a human-size step instead of a dog step. In a minute he'd arrived at the spot and was digging furiously. In another minute he'd hit something hard with his paws. He took a deep breath and blew the sand aside— and there it was.

'A treasure chest!' he cried. 'This is it! The lost treasure of Pegleg Peggy, the pirate from Perth! Oh, joyful day!'

Selby lifted the top of the chest and pointed his torch inside. A blinding sparkle and twinkle and glitter shone back at him.

'The treasure!' he said. 'I've found it! It was true after all! I'm a free dog now! I can't wait to talk to the Trifles and tell them everything!'

Selby grabbed a pawful of jewellery and threw it into the air without knowing why he was doing it. Then he draped a dozen necklaces around his neck and pushed rings on every toe and even put bracelets up and down his legs.

'Wow, look at this!' Selby gasped as he pulled

a jewel-covered crown from the bottom of the pile and put it on his head. 'My very own personal crown! King Selby!'

Selby stood on his hind legs and walked slowly back to the campfire, dropping rings and bracelets everywhere as he went.

'I can't wait to tell the Trifles. Oh boy, oh boy, oh boy!'

Selby paced back and forth by the fire and then stood in the shadows clearing his throat.

'Ahem,' he cleared. 'Aaaaaheeeeem!'

Mrs Trifle's eyes opened and she spotted a necklace and two rings lying in the sand beside her. She reached out and picked them up.

Selby stood nearby smiling a sideways smile and wondering when she'd notice him.

'Darling, wake up!' Mrs Trifle cried, shaking her sleeping husband. 'Look what I've found!'

Dr Trifle woke up slowly and looked at the jewellery.

'I do believe some actors must have camped here,' Mrs Trifle said. 'Look at this jewellery— it's the kind they use in plays.'

'Why, yes,' Dr Trifle said, turning a ring around in his fingers. 'It looks real but it's all fake—completely worthless.' Dr Trifle gave a big laugh. 'Think of it,' he laughed. 'We came to find buried treasure and all we found was costume jewellery!'

Suddenly Mrs Trifle looked over to where Selby stood.

'Goodness me,' she said, rubbing her eyes. 'Did you see what I saw?'

'All I saw was a blur.'

'Me too.'

'Some animal must have dashed into those bushes over there.'

'And that noise,' Mrs Trifle said. 'It sounds like something digging.'

'It's nothing,' Dr Trifle said with a yawn. 'Go back to sleep. It's probably only a possum.'

'That Pegleg Peggy was not only a hopeless actor,' Selby thought as he threw the phoney crown and the rest of the rings and bracelets back in the chest and started filling in the hole. 'She was a hopeless pirate too! What an idiot! Just my luck that all she ever stole was fake costume jewellery!'

SELBY HOME AND HOSED

'Bogusville is in the middle of a crime wave,' Mrs Trifle said to Dr Trifle who was patting Selby, 'and since I'm the mayor, I've called a meeting so we can talk about what to do. You have to come too.'

'A crime wave,' Selby thought. 'That's really creepy. It makes tingles go up my spine.'

'But I was going to wash the car this evening,' Dr Trifle said.

'That's all taken care of,' Mrs Trifle said. 'Vivian is coming to take the car to the car wash while we're out at the meeting.'

'How will Vivian get the car to the car wash?'

'Drive it. What did you think? The keys are in it and it's parked out on the street.'

'You left the keys in the car in the middle of a crime wave? Is that wise?'

'It'll be okay,' Mrs Trifle said. 'No one's ever stolen a car here in Bunya-Bunya Crescent.'

'Well, all right,' said the doctor. 'But who is this Vivian person?'

'Vivian Hanshaw, the car mechanic,' Mrs Trifle explained.

Dr Trifle looked closely at Selby's fur as he patted him.

'The car isn't the only thing that needs a wash,' Dr Trifle said. 'Selby's fur is all flat and dull. I'll have to give him a bath this weekend.'

'Good idea,' said Mrs Trifle. 'I hate it when his fur gets all matted down and horrible.'

As soon as the Trifles were out of the house, Selby—who had just been reading the chapter in *The Art of the Private Investigator* about car theft—began to worry.

'The Trifles are too trusting,' he said. 'Anyone could come along and steal the car. Car thieves are always on the lookout for cars with their keys in them.'

Selby pulled the front curtains apart and peered out into the darkness.

'I'll just keep an eye out to make sure that Vivian what's-her-name—and not some car thief—takes the car.'

No sooner were these words out of his mouth than Selby saw the dark shape of a man walking down Bunya-Bunya Crescent. When he got to the Trifles' car he stopped and peered in through the window.

'Hey, what's he up to?' Selby thought. 'What am I saying—there's nothing wrong with looking in a car window. This is no time to panic. My imagination's running away with me. But, wait! He's opening the door! He's getting into the car! *It's panic time!*'

Before he had time to think, Selby cranked open the window and yelled, 'Get out of there!' in his deepest, most car thief-frightening voice.

The man looked around wondering where the voice had come from.

'I beg your pardon?' he said.

Selby stood there with his paws on the windowsill in full view of the man.

'Crumbs, he's looking right at me now,' Selby thought. 'I've got to stay calm, keep my mouth shut, look innocent, and get away from the window. But how am I going to keep him from stealing the Trifles' car?'

Selby got down and trotted into the study. He picked up the telephone and dialled.

'Bogusville police,' the voice said. 'How may I help you?'

'I'd like to report a car theft,' Selby said.

'Could I have your name and address please?'

'There's no time for that,' Selby said. 'This is an emergency! Just get down here before he steals the car!'

'So the car isn't stolen yet?'

'No, not yet—but he's working on it.'

'Then it's not a car theft.'

'But it's about to be one,' Selby said, listening as the Trifles' car started.

'So what you're actually reporting, technically speaking, is a *theft-in-progress*.'

'Theft, theft-in-progress,' Selby said. 'What's the difference? It's on Bunya-Bunya Crescent and—hey! He's driving away! Is it okay to call it a car theft now? It's a red car! Get down here quickly!'

Selby slammed down the phone and ran out of the house.

'I've got to stop him!' he said, racing down the street. 'I don't know how but at least I've got to try!'

Selby was puffed and about to turn back when he saw the Trifles' car stop for a red light. At the same time a police siren wailed in the distance.

'I've got it,' Selby said as he got closer to the Trifles' car. 'If I can catch him before the light changes, I'll hop on and ride along.'

Just as the light turned green, Selby got to the back of the car, crept quietly up onto its back and then up onto the roof.

'He can't see me up here,' Selby thought. 'Now all I have to do is figure out how to stop him.'

As the car sped off, Selby's feet slid backwards over the slippery surface.

'Oops! This guy's driving like a maniac! I've got to grab hold of something—but there's nothing to grab!'

Selby hooked his claws between the metal strip and the top of the windscreen and lay flat on top of the car as it sped down the street towards the centre of Bogusville. The sound of the siren came closer and closer.

Finally the police car came round the corner, its blue light flashing, the police officer waving out the window.

'Oh, good,' Selby squealed. 'They're about to catch him!'

The Trifles' car slowed and then stopped as

the police car approached. Sergeant Short pointed his torch into the car.

'Oh, it's you, Vivian,' he said. 'I thought you were a car thief. Someone's just stolen a red car and I thought it might be this one.'

'Sorry to disappoint you,' the driver said. 'I'm just taking the Trifles' car to the car wash.'

'Vivian?' Selby thought as he flattened himself even flatter against the top of the car. 'This guy is the mechanic! I forgot that *Vivian* can be a man's name, too! All this time I thought Vivian was a woman!'

'Off you go, then,' Sergeant Short said. Then he added, 'I see you're taking the mayor's dog out for a bit of fresh air.'

The policeman laughed as he tore away.

'The mayor's dog?' Vivian mumbled. 'What's he on about? I think this crime wave is beginning to make the cops crack.'

'That was too close!' Selby thought. 'I'd better get down from here quick before he starts up again!'

Selby was about to climb down when he realised that his claws were caught. He tugged and tugged but they were stuck so tight that he couldn't work them loose. Just then,

Vivian put the car in gear and started off again.

'Oh, no!' Selby thought. 'How will I ever get loose?'

Selby tugged again but it was no use. His claws were wedged so tight that no amount of pulling would pull them loose.

Finally the car slowed and turned into the Clean-as-a-Whistle Car Washatorium.

But instead of getting out of the car, Vivian drove it straight into the Whirligig Auto Washer and Blow-Drying Machine, quickly pushing the buttons that turned it on before rolling up his window again.

'Ouch! That stings my eyes!' Selby thought as a hundred jets of warm soapy water hit him in the face and the huge scrubbing brushes came closer and closer. 'Oh, no! If this contraption doesn't drown me, it'll brush me to death!'

For the next few minutes, Selby was washed, rinsed, waxed and scrubbed to within an inch of his life. Finally the car moved to the end of the machine and he saw the giant whirring buffing wheels coming towards him.

'Those things really *will* kill me!' he thought. 'What does it matter if I give away my secret now? I've got to save my life!'

'Help!' he screamed in plain English. 'Turn this monster off before it skins me alive!'

Above the roar of the Whirligig Auto Buffer and Blow-Drying Machine, Selby heard a faint voice.

'Who said that?' Vivian called.

'I did!' Selby yelled back. 'I'm stuck on top of the car! Just shut the machine off before it kills me! I don't care if you know that I know how to talk.'

'I can't shut it off,' the mechanic yelled back. 'It's got to finish its cycle! Who are you anyway? And how did you get up there? What's this about knowing how to talk?'

'Oh, this is stupid,' Selby mumbled as the buffing wheels crept to within a millimetre of him. 'What a way to go—buffed to death in a car wash!'

Just then, the wheels hit him, pulling his claws loose and hurling him through the air and into the bushes on the other side of the road. Selby watched as the car finally came out of the car wash. Vivian jumped out and looked on top.

'Where are you?' he cried. 'Why, there's nobody here. My goodness me, the police aren't the only ones who are going crackers around here—all this crime-wave stuff must be getting to me too!'

Selby ran home and tore through the hole at the back of the garage and into the lounge-room just as the Trifles came through the front door.

'Just in time,' he thought. 'Now if I can keep from panting, they'll never know I've been running.'

Dr Trifle plonked himself down on the lounge and started patting Selby.

'I take back what I said about Selby needing a bath,' he said.

'But you thought he needed one,' Mrs Trifle said.

'I did, but now his fur is all nice and fluffy. If I didn't know better, I'd think he'd been to a hairdresser or something.'

'You're right,' Mrs Trifle said, patting Selby's head. 'It's as if he's had his fur washed and blown dry. What a laugh!'

'Just my luck,' Selby thought, happy to be alive and back home with the Trifles. 'Right in the middle of a *crime wave*, I end up with a *blow-wave*!'

THE JAWS THAT SNATCH

'That Jerry fellow built us a beautiful swimming pool,' Mrs Trifle said.

She looked at the picture in the Jerry-Built Pools brochure and compared it with the new pool in the Trifles' backyard.

'The only problem is that it's in the wrong place.'

'We can't move it now,' Dr Trifle said. 'You should have said something *before* it was built.'

'I mean it shouldn't be under that tree. I'd hate to have the tree cut down, but it's such a bother scooping leaves out of the water. Look! There goes one now!'

Mrs Trifle pointed to a leaf that drifted down from the top of the tree. It landed in the pool and floated like a tiny boat.

'You were the one who wanted the pool under

the tree so we wouldn't get sunburnt when we were swimming. Remember?'

'I guess I wasn't thinking about the leaves.'

'Don't worry,' Dr Trifle said, giving one of his little scientist smiles, 'I have the perfect answer.'

'You have an answer to leaves?'

'Certainly. Just watch and you'll see how JAWS will solve everything.'

'JAWS? What exactly are JAWS?'

'JAWS isn't a *them*; it's an *it*. It's my new leaf-catching invention. It takes the worry—and the leaves—out of swimming pools.'

'An invention to do that? How exciting! I'll bet JAWS stands for Justifiable Attenuated Water Sucker or some such science talk,' said Mrs Trifle, knowing how her husband named his inventions.

'No, this time it doesn't stand for anything. It's just plain old JAWS, like in your mouth. Watch what happens to that leaf.'

Selby lay nearby in the bushes secretly reading *The Art of the Private Investigator* and watching the Trifles out of the corner of his eye.

'I can't wait till they go out so I can enjoy the new pool,' he thought. 'I'll sit on the edge and dangle my feet in the water to cool off.'

Just as he was thinking this last thought, a giant shark's head suddenly rose from the water, snapped up the leaf in its huge jaws, and disappeared again to the sound of Mrs Trifle's piercing screams.

'Help! Call the police!' she cried. 'Did you see that? There's a monster in our new swimming pool!'

Dr Trifle laughed.

'Nothing to worry about,' he said. 'It's not a real shark. It's just JAWS, my leaf-gobbler.'

Mrs Trifle stepped forward, looking down into the water.

'You mean—that shark is a machine?'

'It's made of fibreglass and has rubberised teeth. I only made it look like a shark to make it more fun.'

'Fun?! It's about as much fun as falling down stairs! Get it out of there this instant. I refuse to swim with that contraption in there.'

'But why?'

'Because it'll mistake me for a leaf and gobble me up, that's why.'

'No, no, you don't understand. It can't possibly eat you.'

'Are you kidding? That thing could eat a car.'

'But darling, it's perfectly safe because it's got EYES,' Dr Trifle explained.

'And teeth the size of bread knives too!' Mrs Trifle said.

'No, EYES aren't the little beady things on the sides of its head. EYES is science talk for Energy-Yield Evaluation System. It's programmed to only gobble up *little* things that come fluttering down—like leaves. You have nothing to worry about. You're not little and you don't flutter. In fact, you're quite large and when you plunge into the water you make quite a large splash.'

'Don't remind me,' Mrs Trifle said, 'but I still don't trust it—EYES or no EYES.'

'I'll show you how safe it is,' Dr Trifle said, leaping into the pool, clothes and all. 'See? It didn't eat me, so it won't eat you. It's perfectly safe.'

'Rubberised or fibreised, I just wish it wasn't so horrible-looking. My goodness!' Mrs Trifle cried, looking at her watch. 'Quick! We have to buy the food for the council barbecue before the shops close! Get yourself back to dry land and get a wriggle on.'

In minutes, Dr Trifle had changed into dry

clothes and the two of them were out the door and driving down Bunya-Bunya Crescent towards the shops.

When they were safely away from the house, Selby crept out of the bushes and picked up the brochure. In it were photos of swimming pools and lots of smiling people diving and swimming and playing in the water.

'This is torture,' he said. 'Here I am, hot and bothered, and the only place to cool off is in a shark-infested swimming pool! I want to be happy and smiley like the people in the pictures. I could dangle my feet in the water but what if that monster gives me the big chomp? It might recognise a people dangly foot when it sees one, but what if it thinks mine is a big furry leaf?'

Selby tiptoed over to the edge of the pool. Finally he plucked up courage and dipped a paw in the water. When nothing happened, he put in two paws and then dipped his head in, too. Down in the cool water was the shimmering shape of the mechanical leaf-crunching monster.

'Dr Trifle was right,' Selby thought. 'This EYES business works for dogs, too. JAWS knows I'm not a leaf.'

Selby grabbed a big cushion and put it at the edge of the pool. Then he lay down with one foot in the water.

'Just my luck that I'm the only non-swimming dog in Australia—and perhaps the world,' he thought as he put on Mrs Trifle's straw hat, her sunglasses, and even plopped a dollop of zinc cream on the end of his nose. 'But this is great. It's better than going to the beach.'

Selby lay there, reading the brochure and, as he did, a breeze came up and sent another leaf down into the water next to his dangling paw. Suddenly Selby saw the shadow of JAWS streaking upwards, breaking the water's surface like a dolphin.

'Oh, no!' Selby cried, pulling his paw out of the water.

The monster machine went spurting upwards in a great arc and then plunged back down to the bottom again with the leaf in its mouth. All of which would have been okay if it hadn't been for the huge wave that rose like a volcano and crashed down over Selby, washing him right into the pool.

'Help!' Selby cried as he scrabbled at the pool's edge. 'Get me out of here! I can't swim!'

But before he could grab anything, the wind sent another leaf and another and another into the water around him. JAWS broke the surface again and again, knocking Selby about in the choppy water.

'Stop it! You great phoney fibreglass fish!' Selby gasped. 'You're going to drown me!'

Selby thrashed about as JAWS disappeared to the bottom again with the last leaf clamped firmly in its teeth.

'If only I can stay afloat for a couple of seconds,' Selby thought. 'If I keep up the thrashing—*gulp*—I might get to the side of the pool!'

Selby slapped the water with his paws, splashing water in every direction and moving slightly sideways towards the edge of the pool. He gasped and sputtered, his head dipping below the surface and then bobbing up for another gulp of air.

Slowly he moved to within whisker-distance of the edge.

'If I can only—*gasp*—get a paw—*gulp*—up on the side of the—*glug*—pool—' he sputtered.

Suddenly, just as he hooked a paw up and over the edge of the pool and was about to leap out of the water, he looked up to see one last lone leaf come fluttering down towards him.

'Oh, no!' he cried, losing his toenail grip and slipping away from the edge. 'As soon as that thing hits the water, this stupid synthetic sea-serpent will drown me for sure! I've got to keep it from landing!'

Selby drew in a deep breath and blew upwards, sending the leaf back up in the air. The first blow was followed by another and another as the leaf hovered above his head, not knowing whether to flutter up or flutter down.

'I can't keep up this blowing forever!' Selby thought. 'I'm already so dizzy that I'm about to faint!'

The leaf teetered back and forth, side to side, fluttering up, then floating down. Then suddenly Selby's blowing weakened and the leaf took a sudden dive, smack onto the zinc cream on the end of his nose.

'I've caught it!' Selby yelled. 'Thank goodness it's stuck to my nose. It can't hit the water now! *Yiiipppeee*!'

But Selby spoke too soon—and too loudly— because the breath of his *yiiipppeee*! blew the leaf off the end of his nose and smack into the water beside him.

'Oh, no!' Selby shrieked as JAWS came charging out of the depths, smacking him from below as it sped towards the leaf.

The next thing Selby knew he was flying through the air, landing on the grass beside the pool. As he hit the ground, Mrs Trifle, who had just come home, tore out of the house and scooped Selby up in her arms.

'Did you see that?!' she screamed at Dr Trifle. 'Your JAWS-thing actually saved Selby's life! He must have fallen into the pool. It knocked him back out again! It not only gobbles leaves, it rescues drowning pets! What a marvellous invention!'

'I told you JAWS would be useful,' Dr Trifle said, feeling very proud of himself. 'Sometimes my own inventions surprise even me.'

'JAWS, SCHMAWS,' Selby thought as he coughed some water out of his lungs. 'I'm just happy to be a PUP—and I don't mean a young dog. PUP is dog talk for a Pleasantly Un-drowned Pooch.'

SELBY SUPERSNOUT

It all began the day that Selby read the chapter in *The Art of the Private Investigator* on using dogs to sniff out clues.

'I'd be a hopeless sniffer-dog,' Selby thought as he sniffed his way around the house. 'I couldn't find a rotten fish in a room full of roses. And all this dust makes me feel like a four-legged vacuum cleaner. *Achoooo*!'

That afternoon Dr and Mrs Trifle received an invitation to the launch of a fabulously expensive new perfume made by the famous perfume-maker, Pierre de Paris of the House of Pierre Perfumerie.

'I know they launch ships,' said Dr Trifle, 'but I didn't know they launched perfumes.'

'It's really just a big party to tell everyone about the perfume,' Mrs Trifle explained.

'They've hired the movie theatre for the evening. This new perfume is called Composure.'

'Composure? What an odd name,' Dr Trifle said. 'Why don't they call it Morning Rose or Evening Daffodil—something that smells like something?'

'These days perfumes have much more interesting names like Quest, and React, and Lightning, and Composure. The names have nothing to do with the smell anymore.'

'If you ask me, I think it's all very silly,' Dr Trifle said. 'People should spend their money on more useful things.'

'It's really just a bit of fun,' Mrs Trifle said. 'And I'm kind of looking forward to going.'

'Well, I reckon it isn't that difficult to make perfumes,' Dr Trifle said. 'I'll bet I could whip up a lovely fragrance in no time.'

'I think you'll find that it's not that easy.'

'We'll see about that,' Dr Trifle said, heading for his workroom.

'Perfumes,' Selby thought. 'I don't understand them. Why can't people just smell like people? Why do they waste so much money trying to smell like something else? I mean, I'm a dog and I smell like a dog. What's wrong with that?'

* * *

For the next few days the most revolting smells drifted out of Dr Trifle's workroom. Finally, Dr Trifle appeared, smiling, and holding three small bottles.

'Ta-da!' he sang. 'The House of Trifle is proud to bring you Smell-O-Scents, a new concept in perfumes.'

'A new concept?' Mrs Trifle said, very suspiciously. 'What *are* you talking about?'

'The thing about ordinary perfumes,' Dr Trifle said, 'is that they usually just smell nice. They have the scent of roses, or jasmine, or camellias.'

'What do yours smell like?'

'My Smell-O-Scents don't smell like any one thing. They *remind* you of places—tropical islands, mountain peaks, rivers. They don't just cover up people smells.'

'I'm not sure I'd know the smell of a tropical island if I sniffed one,' Mrs Trifle said.

'That's because they don't have just one smell. They have lots of smells all together. Some of the smells are horrible and some are nice. When you mix them together in the right amounts something wonderful happens.'

'Are you talking about scents? Or are you

talking *non*-scents?' Mrs Trifle laughed. 'Get it? Scents? Nonsense?'

'Yes, very funny, dear,' Dr Trifle said, holding up one of his bottles. 'But have a whiff of this.'

Mrs Trifle sniffed it and suddenly a smile spread across her lips.

'Mmmmmmm,' she said. 'That's very interesting. It reminds me of something.'

'What?' Dr Trifle asked eagerly.

'Rafting down a river.'

'Smell-O-Stream,' Dr Trifle said. 'That's what I've named it. You see, it works!'

By now Selby had made his way quietly up to Mrs Trifle's side and had sneaked a secret sniff.

'Crikey!' he thought. 'It's true! It reminds me of wild rivers and forests. Dr Trifle is very clever.'

'Here, try another one,' Dr Trifle said.

Mrs Trifle dabbed a drop of the next perfume on her wrist and sniffed it.

'Deserts,' she said. 'Dry, wind-swept places. Red rocks with bits of blue grass growing between them. And lots of sand.'

'She's right,' Selby thought. 'That's what it reminds me of too!'

'Smell-O-Sand,' Dr Trifle said. 'And now try this one.'

'Tropical islands come to mind,' Mrs Trifle said. 'That's the best one.'

'Smell-O-Surf,' Dr Trifle said proudly.

Selby put his nose close to the bottle and drew a deep breath and closed his eyes.

'I feel like I'm lying on a yacht,' he thought, 'anchored off palm-covered islands. People are bringing me plates of delicious food. Dr Trifle isn't just clever—he's a genius! These Smell-O-Scents are fantastic!'

'Goodness, look at Selby,' Mrs Trifle said. 'I think he likes that one. I guess we'll never know what it reminds him of.'

'I'd better get back to work on Smell-O-Snow, my mountain perfume,' Dr Trifle said. 'But I think I'll take a bottle of the Smell-O-Surf along to the launch tonight to show these House of Pierre people. Maybe they'll want to buy the formula from me.'

That evening, the Trifles and Selby were met by Pierre de Paris himself as they entered the Bogusville Bijou Theatre.

'Good evening,' he said as hundreds of people filed past them. 'I am told that you're the mayor of this lovely town.'

'Yes, and this is my husband, Dr Trifle,' Mrs Trifle said. 'He has a little something to show you—his new perfume.'

'A perfume-maker in Bogusville? This is impossible!'

'I'm just an amateur; a dabbler,' Dr Trifle said. 'Or, should I say, a *dabber*, since we're talking about perfume.'

'How very interesting,' the man said stiffly. 'But show me later. And please, no dogs.'

'Selby will behave himself,' Mrs Trifle said.

'It is not the behaviour but the odour,' Pierre said, pinching his nose with his fingers. 'Little doggies smell like . . . little doggies. He will cause confusion to the noses.'

'Confusion to the noses? Doggie odour?' Selby thought. 'What does this perfumed poncy pants want me to smell like: an ostrich?'

'Selby, I'm afraid you'll have to stay here,' Mrs Trifle said, giving Selby a pat. 'Sorry.'

'Oh, great,' thought Selby as the Trifles went into the theatre. 'Why couldn't they have just left me at home? I could have watched TV or read a book or something. I'll tell you what, I'm not sitting around out here.'

When everyone was seated, the music began,

the lights dimmed, and Selby crept into the hall.

'Nobody will notice me back here,' he thought. 'And I can watch the show just like anyone else.'

For the next half hour one beautifully dressed model after another came to the middle of the stage, turned around twice and then walked off again. Each time another model appeared, Pierre's assistants sprayed a different perfume in the air and Pierre said its name slowly and deeply into his microphone: 'Suspense,' he said. 'Shadows' . . . 'Melancholy'. . . . 'Excitement.'

Finally it was time for the big moment. The hall went completely black, a drum played a drum roll and suddenly the air was filled with a different perfume. A murmur of excitement went through the audience and then the spotlight fell on Pierre, standing in the middle of the stage.

'And now, the moment we have all been waiting for!' he said. 'The House of Pierre proudly brings you—Composure!'

'Composure?' Selby thought, sniffing a big sniff. 'It smells more like compost. Smell-O-Surf is so much better than any of these Pong de Paris perfumes. It's all a big con.'

When the clapping died down, Pierre cried,

'Tonight, ladies and gentlemen, and tonight only, we have decided to slash our price and give you Composure at the special, once-only, low, low figure of only ninety-nine dollars and ninety-five cents!'

'One hundred smackeroos!' Selby thought. 'That's outrageous! All that money for a tiny bottle of smelly liquid! What a rip-off! Forget the perfume; this Pierre guy is really beginning to get up my nose!'

But before these thoughts were out of Selby's brain a few people dashed up to the stage and began buying the perfume.

'It would almost be worth giving away my secret just to be able to shout out, "Don't buy that muck; it's a waste of money!" Hey, now wait a minute! Hold the show! I know what I'll do.'

Selby crept down under the seats till he was under Dr Trifle's seat. Very slowly, and without the doctor noticing, Selby put his snout down in Dr Trifle's jacket pocket and grabbed the bottle of Smell-O-Surf gently in his teeth. In a minute he had placed the bottle on a table at the back of the theatre and had the cap off.

'Now all I have to do is move the table over in front of the air conditioner,' Selby said, pushing the table, 'and I'll give them a whiff of something really good.'

Selby stepped outside the door again as the smell of tropical islands spread through the theatre. Suddenly there were *ooooos* and *aaaaaahs* all around.

'What is that heavenly smell?' someone cried.

'It reminds me of ocean breezes and coral reefs,' someone else said. 'I feel like I've just gone on holidays.'

'Forget the Composure stuff, Mr Pierre,' a woman said. 'Where can we buy some of this?'

Dr Trifle searched his pockets for the bottle. Soon one of Pierre's assistants located the bottle of Smell-O-Surf, sniffed it and put the lid back on.

'Whose perfume is this?' Pierre demanded.

'I'm terribly sorry,' Dr Trifle said. 'I'm afraid this one's mine.'

'Yours?' Pierre said. 'Why did you want to ruin my beautiful launch?!'

'I—I didn't,' Dr Trifle said. 'I don't know how it got there. Honestly, I don't.'

Selby chuckled to himself as everyone crowded around Dr Trifle.

'Where can we buy this beautiful fragrance?' they demanded.

'I don't have any more,' Dr Trifle said. 'Only what's in that bottle. I guess I could make some more though. It's really not difficult to make.'

'Get out of here, all of you ungrateful people!' Pierre screamed. 'You are stupid, uncouth country people! You know nothing! I have wasted my time with you! Out! Out!'

Everyone filed out of the theatre. Pierre was standing stiffly in the doorway as Dr and Mrs Trifle went out.

'We're terribly sorry,' Mrs Trifle said. 'We really don't know what happened.'

'I will tell you one thing,' Pierre said. 'I am never coming back to this terrible town!'

'I quite understand,' Dr Trifle said politely, adding, 'Oh, by the way, may I have my perfume back?'

'I don't know where it is,' Pierre said.

'But one of your assistants had it,' Mrs Trifle said.

'Then it is a mystery,' Pierre said, blowing his nose in his silk handkerchief. 'He must have thrown it away.'

'Never mind,' Dr Trifle said, 'I can make some more.'

'That guy's lying,' Selby thought. 'One of

these guys has Dr Trifle's perfume. Now they'll take it back to their laboratory and figure out how to make it. He's just stolen Dr Trifle's formula! And now Pierre will make grillions of dollars from it! Crumbs—and it's all my fault.'

Just then, Selby smelled a faint smell of Smell-O-Surf. For a second he was back in the tropics lying on the beach. In his daydream he got up, stretched, and looked up at the coconuts in the palms above him.

'I'd love a nice sip of coconut milk,' he thought. 'Maybe I'll just climb up and pick a coconut.'

In his mind, Selby leapt halfway up a palm, only to have it fall to the ground under his weight.

Selby came back to reality with a start.

'Get that savage dog off me!' a voice cried. 'He's trying to kill me!'

Selby opened his eyes and there was Pierre lying on his back on the floor under him.

'Goodness, Selby,' Mrs Trifle said. 'Get off that man. What's got into you?'

Mrs Trifle was pulling Selby back by the collar when suddenly Dr Trifle's perfume bottle rolled out of Pierre's pocket.

'Just as I suspected,' Selby thought. 'That scoundrel had it all the time!'

'I believe we've just located the bottle,' Dr Trifle said, picking it up. 'Come along, Selby. I think you've solved our little mystery.'

'So I have,' Selby thought. 'Come to think of it, maybe I'm not such a bad sniffer-dog, after all.'

SELBY UNSTUCK

'Look! Come quickly!' Mrs Trifle cried.

Dr Trifle came dashing into the study with Selby right behind him.

'What is it, dear?' the doctor asked.

'A great discovery!' Mrs Trifle said, holding up an old postcard. 'I found this in the middle of that book about Canada. I suspect that your great, great, great-grandfather, Fred Trifle, wrote it to your great, great, great-grandmother, Matilda, before they were married.'

Dr Trifle held up the postcard and read it:

September 15, 1857

Dear Matilda,
The weather is here, wish you were beautiful.
Ha, ha. Great joke, isn't it? See you soon.

Love, Fred

Dr Trifle looked puzzled as he re-read the card.

'Yes, very interesting,' he said, finally, 'but that's the oldest, corniest postcard joke in the world. Instead of writing, "The weather is beautiful, wish you were here," he wrote "The weather is here, wish you were beautiful." Get it?'

'Of course I get it,' Mrs Trifle sighed. 'You used to write it on every postcard you sent me before we were married, remember?'

'Did I?'

'You did.'

'Come to think of it, I did,' the doctor chuckled.

'Well, it wasn't funny then and it isn't funny now.'

'But you used to tell me how funny it was.'

'I was being polite,' Mrs Trifle said. 'But it isn't the message on this postcard I wanted you to see; it's the stamp.'

Dr Trifle looked at the stamp.

'Hmmm,' he hmmmed. 'It's a triangle with a picture of flying ducks on it and it says "Newfoundland" and "Two Pence" on the bottom. It's a strange one, all right. It could be worth a fortune.'

'A *double* fortune,' Mrs Trifle said. 'The ducks were printed upside down by mistake. An old stamp with a mistake on it must be very, very rare and very, very valuable. Let's take it to a stamp expert and see how much it's worth.'

'Speaking of corny old jokes,' Dr Trifle said. 'Our comedian friend Gary Gaggs is a bit of a stamp-nut and we're going to his comedy show tomorrow night, remember? Maybe he can come back here afterwards and tell us what the stamp is worth.'

'Good idea.'

That night, when the Trifles were safely in bed, Selby crept into the study and had a good look at the stamp.

'What a great find!' he thought. 'I wonder if the Trifles are going to sell it? I'd sell it in a second! Wow, all that money! Goody, goody! What a great holiday they could have!'

The next day everyone in Bogusville had heard about the rare stamp. Soon there were newspaper people and TV crews knocking at the door to interview the Trifles and to take pictures of the postcard.

'I don't like everyone knowing that there's something so valuable in the house,' Dr Trifle said that evening. 'Someone might break in and steal it. And we can't insure it because we still don't know how much it's worth. Maybe we should have kept it secret for a few days.'

'Don't worry, dear. I'll put it in our bank vault tomorrow. In the meantime, I'm sure it'll be fine right here in this book.'

That evening the Trifles went to Gary Gaggs' comedy show and Selby stayed at home.

'This rare stamp business was so exciting at first,' Selby thought, 'but now it gives me the shivers. I hope nothing happens while the Trifles are away.'

No sooner did these words trickle through Selby's brain than there was the crash and tinkle of breaking glass in the other room.

'What was that?' Selby wondered. 'Could it be someone breaking in?'

It could and it was: into the study climbed two men wearing black burglar masks. Selby ducked out of sight around the corner before they noticed him.

'Is this the place?' one of the burglars asked the other.

'Yeah, this is it all right,' the other said.

'Okay, let's get to work and find that stamp.'

Selby heard the burglars pulling books from the shelves.

'I found the postcard!' one of the men said, finally. 'We're rich! Come on, let's get out of here!'

'Oh, no!' Selby thought. 'The Trifles are about to lose the stamp! I can't let this happen!'

Suddenly Selby remembered an article he'd seen about burglaries and burglar alarms.

'Some of the best burglar alarms are the ones that have recorded voices,' he remembered. 'They yell things out and the burglars think that someone's at home and go running off.'

Just as the burglars turned to go back out the window, Selby yelled out the first thing that popped into his head: 'All right, you two! This is the police! Come out of that room with your hands up!'

'The cops!' one of the burglars whispered.

'It can't be!' the other one whispered.

'It is. They must be in the lounge room.'

'Okay, don't shoot! We give up!' the first one called out.

Slowly the burglars came into the lounge room

with their hands in the air. One of them was holding the postcard.

'Oops! I did it wrong,' Selby thought. 'I should have just told them to drop the postcard and get out! What do I do now?'

The burglars looked around the room and then one of them put his hands down and started laughing. He went over to Selby and patted him on the head.

'What's so funny?' the other one asked.

'You, you dummy. Can't you see there's no one here but this dog?'

'So where are the cops?'

'There aren't any cops. It's just one of those stupid burglar alarms. Someone put the wrong message on it. They should have said, "Get out before I call the police," or something like that. What a ninny!'

Suddenly Selby remembered something else from the burglar article.

'The best burglar alarm is a dog,' he remembered. 'Hey, That's me! I'm a dog! I'm a burglar alarm! I should be barking and snarling and biting and all those other dog-like things! But wait, if I do that now, they'll run off with the stamp! Why didn't I do it *before* they found the stamp?'

But Selby noticed that the burglar with the postcard was holding it right next to his nose as he patted him. Slowly and secretly Selby's tongue slid out and touched a corner of the stamp. In a moment he'd wet it through and had a loose corner of the stamp in his teeth. He pulled gently, and then he pulled not so gently, and finally he gave it a yank and a jerk and the stamp slipped into his mouth and was safely hidden under his tongue.

'Hey! The dog's got the stamp!' the burglar yelled. 'Grab him!'

Selby turned and let out a flurry of barking and growling so ferocious that it even frightened him.

'Hey! This dog's going to kill us!' the other burglar yelled. 'Let's get out of here!'

The two men ran back into the study and dived through the window as Selby ripped at their trousers.

'That was good fun!' Selby squealed when the burglars were safely out of sight. 'Now all I have to do is glue the stamp back on the postcard and put the books back on the shelves. The Trifles will know that someone broke their window but at least they'll have their stamp.'

Selby opened his mouth to spit the stamp out but nothing came out. He moved his tongue around and around searching for it and then went to the mirror, opened his mouth and gazed in.

'It's gone!' he cried. 'While I was barking and growling, I swallowed the stamp! By now it's completely dissolved. Oh woe, woe, woe! Why couldn't it have been a coin instead of a stamp! At least a coin would come out the other end in one piece!'

That evening the Trifles arrived home with Gary

Gaggs who made straight for Selby and began patting him.

'I love your dog,' he said. 'I used to have a dog myself once. It was a black dog—but then again, it wasn't a black dog.'

'How is that possible?' Mrs Trifle said.

'It's simple: he was a *grey*hound,' Gary said, pumping his arms up and down, strutting around like a rooster and saying, 'Woo woo woo!' as he always did when he made a joke.

'That's very good,' Dr Trifle said. 'You never stop, do you?'

'But seriously, folks,' Gary went on, 'his name was Dale. I tried to take him up in a plane with me but he wouldn't go. You see he wasn't an *Aire*dale. Woo woo woo! But speaking of stamps, you do know the difference between a woman and a stamp, don't you?'

'Well, I think so,' Mrs Trifle said, wondering why there was a draught coming from the study.

'One of them's a *female*,' Gary said, 'and the other one's a *mail fee*. Woo woo woo!'

Just then, the Trifles noticed the broken window and the stampless postcard lying on the floor.

'Someone's stolen the stamp,' Mrs Trifle

cried. 'We were so silly! Why didn't we just take it with us?'

'Calm down,' Gary Gaggs said. 'From the way you described it, the stamp was just a Newfoundland Tuppenny Triangle. I'm afraid they aren't worth anything. They printed tonnes of them.'

'But this one had the ducks printed upside down,' Dr Trifle explained.

'Worthless,' Gary said. 'They were *all* printed with the ducks upside down. Well—almost all. The stamps with the ducks rightside up are the valuable ones—there are only three of them left in the whole world.'

'Well, thank goodness for that,' Dr Trifle sighed. 'I guess some burglar is in for a big disappointment.'

Gary turned over the postcard, read the message and then burst out laughing.

'Get a look at this!' he said. '"The weather is here, wish you were beautiful." That's great!'

Mrs Trifle frowned.

'Haven't you heard it before?' she asked. 'It's the oldest postcard joke in the world.'

'Of course I've heard it,' Gary said. 'The point is that this was written in 1857. It's probably the first time that joke was ever used. Your great, great, great-grandfather probably made it up! I'm going to recommend that the International Jokes Library in Gulargambone buy this postcard for their collection.'

'What an interesting idea,' Dr Trifle said. 'Do you suppose they'll pay us a fortune?'

'I doubt it,' Gary Gaggs said. 'But they'll probably pay you enough to buy a decent burglar alarm.'

'A burglar alarm,' Mrs Trifle said. 'What a good idea.'

'Burglar alarm, schmurglar alarm,' Selby thought as he licked some trouser threads out of his teeth. 'What you need is what you've already got: a good old barking, biting, and *thinking* dog—me!'

SMOOCHY POOCH

'She's the most beautiful dog I've ever seen,' Selby thought as he and the Trifles sat in front of the TV watching their weekly episode of *Bella Barktalk, Crimefighter*. 'She may only be a cartoon, but she makes my little heart flutter like a butterfly.'

As the programme began, Bella was standing in front of the police officers of her Special Squad giving them their orders. But the Trifles' viewing was suddenly interrupted by a knock at their door.

'I wonder who that could be?' Mrs Trifle said.

'That'll be Aunt Jetty,' Dr Trifle answered. 'I'll get it.'

'Oh, no,' Selby thought. 'It's bad enough that she stays with the Trifles when she's in Bogusville, but why does she have to come in just when my favourite show is on?'

Selby watched as Bella planned the raid on the crooks' hideout.

'Be careful,' she told her officers. 'This will be dangerous, but if you all follow my orders you'll be safe. Got it?'

'Yes, captain!' the officers all shouted, then ran to their police cars and roared away.

Selby looked up as Aunt Jetty followed Dr Trifle into the room.

'What's this stupid programme you're watching?' she asked. 'Good heavens; it's a cartoon!'

'It's very good,' Mrs Trifle said. 'And it's quite serious really.'

'But they're all dogs,' Aunt Jetty protested. 'How can it be serious?'

'They're really like people,' Dr Trifle said. 'They think and act just like humans. They talk and everything.'

'Talking dogs, poobah!' Aunt Jetty said, looking at Selby. 'What will they think of next?'

'Sit down and watch for a few minutes,' Mrs Trifle said. 'I guarantee you'll be hooked.'

Selby lay on the floor next to the lounge, behind the Trifles' chairs, giving Aunt Jetty his toothiest, most lip-curling look.

'Old Horrible isn't about to bite me again, is he?' Aunt Jetty said, pushing Selby out of her way with her foot before sitting down. 'What a disgusting little creature he is.'

'You'll be perfectly safe,' Mrs Trifle assured her sister.

'If he tries anything unfriendly I'll have his guts for garters—mark my words.'

'Oh, keep quiet you great gangling galumph,' Selby thought. 'I'm trying to watch *Bella Barktalk*.'

Bella silently signalled her officers to surround the crooks' hideaway. One by one they spread out around the old building. Then

Bella's long-time partner, Frank, turned to her.

'I'm scared,' he said. 'I've never been scared before but I am now.'

'But we've done this a hundred times before,' Bella told him. 'If we stick to the plan, we'll be okay.'

'Not this time,' Frank said. 'Something's wrong, I can feel it. I say we don't go in. This time they know we're out here.'

Bella looked deep into his eyes.

'Frank, we can't stop now,' she said.

'Why doesn't she ever tell him that she loves him?' Selby thought. 'It's so obvious. And he loves her too. But they never ever tell each other.'

'Please trust me,' Bella told her partner. 'Trust me.'

Bella gave the signal but before her Special Squad could go in, guns blazed from every window of the building sending Bella's officers running for cover. Bella dashed towards the building but turned to see Frank fall to the ground.

'Frank!' she cried. 'No, Frank!'

In the next scene, Bella was standing next to Frank's hospital bed, clutching a bouquet of flowers. He lay there unconscious.

'Frank, Frank,' Bella whimpered, the tears streaming down her face. 'I can't live without you. It was my fault. I never should have given that order.'

But as she reached out to grasp his hand, the machine above his bed that had been going *ping ping ping* suddenly made one last long ringing noise.

'No, Frank!' Bella screamed as nurse-dogs and doctor-dogs ran from everywhere, pounding on his chest to restart his heart. 'Please don't die.'

The head nurse pulled the curtains around Frank's bed as they worked to revive him. Bella walked slowly away, dropping the bouquet of flowers in the hospital corridor.

Selby sniffed a little sniffle and then he heard the Trifles sniffle too. Just then, Aunt Jetty burst out laughing.

'What rubbish!' she said. 'Who cares about a dying dog? What a joke! I mean it's not like he's a human or anything.'

'I wish she'd just shut up,' Selby thought. 'If only I could block her out—pretend she's not here. She's ruining the whole show!'

Aunt Jetty kept talking and laughing but Selby used his powers of total concentration to pretend that he was there with Bella Barktalk in the hospital instead of at home with Aunt Jetty.

Suddenly the scene changed to a grassy field. Bella was sitting on a rock pulling petals from a daisy.

'She's such a wonderful dog,' Selby thought. 'She's tough, of course, but she's tender and sensitive at the same time. Why can't I find a dog like that? Oh, how I wish I wasn't the only talking dog in Australia and, perhaps, the world.'

Mrs Trifle blew her nose in her handkerchief as Bella's tears streamed down her cheeks.

'Captain Barktalk?' a voice said.

Bella wheeled around and Frank was standing there, smiling, and still wearing his hospital pyjamas and bandages.

'Frank!' Bella cried. 'It's you! You're alive!'

'Dear, sweet Bella,' Frank laughed, throwing his arms around her. 'It's all right. I'm going to live.'

'Oh, Frank!' Bella whispered, clutching him tighter.

'And from now on, I'm going to live with you.'

Bella drew back slightly.

'Do you mean—?' she began.

'Yes, darling,' he said. 'Will you marry me?'

'Oh yes, Frank. Yes. Yes. Yes!'

Selby's powers of concentration were so great that for a moment he was actually kissing Bella himself. He could feel the warmth of her lips and her body pressing against his. He hugged her tighter and then slowly opened his eyes—only to see two big startled eyes looking back at him.

'Bella?' he thought.

But these weren't the soft eyes of his beloved dog-hero. These weren't the eyes of the tough but tender dog of his dreams. These were the horrified saucer-sized eyes of Aunt Jetty.

'Help!' Selby thought, his lips still pressing against hers. 'What have I done? I've kissed Aunt Jetty, that's what I've done! Help!'

Aunt Jetty's shock at Selby's big wet kiss had been so great that she'd sat there rigid as a tree-trunk while Selby slowly pulled his mouth from hers, released her from his grip, and stepped down from the lounge.

'Oh, yuck!' Aunt Jetty screamed, wiping her lips with a handkerchief. 'Icky poo!'

Dr and Mrs Trifle turned around in their chairs.

'What's wrong?' Mrs Trifle asked.

'He did it! I knew he'd do something, and he did!'

'Did he bite you?' Dr Trifle asked.

'Bite me? No. He slobbered all over my lips! I'm going to die of some dreaded dog disease! Call a doctor! I need anti-dog drops, quick! Get me to a hospital! Help!'

'Surely he was just giving you a friendly lick,' Mrs Trifle said, watching Selby crawl through the flap in the back door and out into the yard. 'He's a very affectionate dog. He probably just likes you, that's all.'

'Like her? Good grief!' Selby thought as he spat into the bushes. 'I just got the worst fright of my life! One minute I'm kissing my dream-dog and the next thing I know she turns into my worst nightmare!'

PHANTOM FOOTPRINTS

'Wouldn't you rather go out to dinner tonight?' Dr Trifle said as he cut up the vegetables for the meal he was about to cook.

'You've forgotten about my symphony,' Mrs Trifle said. 'We don't have time.'

'Your symphony? Since when are you writing symphonies?'

'It's not really *my* symphony; it's a new work by Jango Phoot. We're rehearsing it tonight and then performing it tomorrow.'

'Who exactly is *we*?'

'The BSDS.'

'The BSDS?'

'The Bogusville Song and Dance Society. Sometimes I wonder if you listen to a word I say. This is a really big event. People from all over the world will be coming tomorrow night. It's Phoot's first major work in ten years.'

'So who is this Phoot fellow?'

'He's Australia's most famous composer of MM.'

'MM?'

'Maximal Music. And he was born in Bogusville.'

'Oh, *that* Jango Phoot,' Dr Trifle said. 'Doesn't he write that plinkity plunkity kind of music that you can't hum or whistle?'

'It's not plinkity plunkity anymore. It's more crashity bangity,' Mrs Trifle said. 'Especially this new piece. It's called *The Great Chicken Disaster Symphony*. It's based on something that happened when he was a young man. His truckload of chickens overturned and all the chickens escaped. It's very personal music.'

'Hmmm, *The Great Chicken Disaster Symphony*. Very interesting, but why does he want to perform it in Bogusville?'

'Because country people are friendly people.'

'We are?'

'Yes. In the city there are people who hate him. Some of them come to his concerts just to boo and hiss and carry on. Once someone even threw a bucket of tomato sauce all over the audience in the middle of a performance. That could never happen here.'

'Let's hope not,' Dr Trifle said. 'So will you be singing or playing an instrument?'

'I'll be screaming and clucking and singing the part of the principal pullet.'

'A pullet? Isn't that a young chicken?'

'Yes, darling, and you'll love my screaming too,' Mrs Trifle said proudly. 'It sounds just like tyres screeching. Do you want a demonstration?'

'I think I'd rather wait for opening night and be surprised, thank you all the same,' said Dr Trifle who was cracking eggs into a bowl and thinking of escaping chickens.

'I'll take Selby along to the rehearsal,' Mrs Trifle said, 'he needs a walk. I trust the meal will be ready VS.'

'VS?'

'Very soon.'

'Yes, of course, dear. You go and get ready.'

'*The Great Chicken Disaster Symphony*,' Selby thought as he lay behind the lounge listening to Dr and Mrs Trifle's conversation. 'I'm not sure that it's my kind of music but it'll be great to see the BSDS rehearse.'

* * *

That night Selby and Mrs Trifle made their way in the rain to Bogusville Hall. Selby sat at the back of the hall watching as the grey-haired Jango Phoot conducted the Bogusville Song and Dance Society by waving a bent windscreen wiper.

Constable Long smashed bottles, Phil Philpot broke up a wooden barrel with an axe, Postie Paterson beat on a bathtub with a hammer, Melanie Mildew made hideous scratching noises by running her long fingernails down a blackboard, and the rest of the BSDS (including Mrs Trifle) clucked, screamed, honked horns and made the noise of police sirens.

'I don't know if this Maximal Music sounds good,' Selby thought as he covered his ears, 'but it sure is fun to watch!'

Finally, the symphony came to a great crashing end.

'Take ten!' the composer called. 'Well, what did you people think of it?'

There was silence for a moment and then Phil Philpot said, 'I think I messed up some of those wood-splitting sounds.'

'That part sounded good to me,' Postie Paterson said. 'But my bathtub is a little out of tune. You don't suppose we could find an E flat bathtub?'

'I may have spoiled the end bit when I broke my fingernail,' Melanie Mildew said. 'I'll have to glue on a false one for opening night.'

'Well, I liked it,' Constable Long said. 'It's much better than that plinkity plunkity music you used to write.'

Jango Phoot sighed.

'Thank you for your comments,' he said. 'I really don't know what to think. I'm so nervous about tomorrow night. Anyway, now that it's stopped raining, I'll take a walk around the block. See you soon.'

While the composer was out of the hall, Mrs Trifle and the others talked about the symphony.

'He's really captured the sound of a truck crash, hasn't he?' Postie Paterson said.

'It sounds just like recess at school on a windy day,' said Camilla Bonser, the librarian at Bogusville Primary School, 'with all the kids going crazy.'

'I don't think Mr Phoot is happy with his symphony,' Mrs Trifle said. 'But then, I guess I'd be nervous too if it was my new symphony and all these important people were coming to hear it.'

Selby was listening to all this when suddenly

he noticed something sail through one of the high windows in the hall and then come shooting down to the floor.

'Look! It's a paper plane,' Constable Long said, 'with a note on it.'

'I'll take that,' said Camilla Bonser who was used to grabbing notes away from the kids at school. 'It says "Cancel tomorrow's performance if you know what's good for you," and it's signed "The Tomato Sauce Phantom". I wonder what it means?'

'Let's see who threw it!' Constable Long said.

Everyone, including Selby, ran outside and into the car park, but there was no one there.

'Footprints!' Mrs Trifle said, pointing to the tracks in the mud that stretched across the field. 'Look! I see him way over there, standing on the footpath!'

'I think you're mistaken,' Constable Long said. 'That's not the culprit—that's Jango.'

'But the footprints are going straight towards him.'

'If you look carefully, you'll see that they're going in the opposite direction,' the policeman said. 'They're coming towards us—*away* from him.'

'Oh, so they are,' Mrs Trifle said. 'Yoohoo, Mr Phoot! Could you come here please?'

The composer made his way across the muddy field.

'Someone threw this note through the window,' Camilla explained.

The composer took the note and read it.

'So that's what he was up to,' he said. 'I saw a man run towards the hall and then throw something towards the window.'

'Where'd he go?' Constable Long asked.

'After he threw this, he ran out the driveway to the street, hopped into a car and drove away,' the composer said. 'And I thought I'd be safe here in Bogusville. I guess I'll have to cancel tomorrow's performance.'

'You can't just cancel,' Phil Philpot said. 'What about all the people who are coming?'

'I can't risk having tomato sauce thrown on them—or worse. There's no telling what these so-called music-lovers might do. I can't put them in danger.'

'It's very sad,' Selby thought as he and Mrs Trifle walked home. 'Ten years of work down the drain. And now he'll probably never write music again—plinkity plunkity or crashity bangity.'

'I know you don't know what's happening, Selby,' Mrs Trifle said, 'but this is all very sad. You're so lucky to be in your simple little doggy world and not in our complicated people-world.'

'Simple, schmimple,' Selby thought. 'I only wish I could find the guy who threw that note.'

That night, when he couldn't sleep, Selby suddenly remembered the chapter in *The Art of the Private Investigator* about footprints.

'I should have studied the footprints,' he thought. 'What if the culprit was wearing a shoe with a chip out of the heel? What if he used a walking-stick? There might have been an important clue.'

With this, Selby got up, crept out of the house, and ran all the way back to Bogusville Hall.

'Hmmm,' Selby thought as he studied the footprints. 'Nothing unusual here. No chips. No walking-sticks. Just plain old footprints. In fact,' he said, looking over at the footprints that Jango Phoot had made, 'they're kind of like Jango's.'

Selby put his nose down closer to the mud.

'Hey, hold the show! They're *exactly* like Jango's! But they can't be! Jango was walking around the block on the road. Unless . . . unless

Jango *wasn't* walking around the block. Maybe he scribbled the note, made it into a paper plane, threw it, and then ran *backwards* across that field to where we saw him.'

Selby looked around the car park.

'That explains why he left muddy footprints in the car park when he came towards us but there are no muddy footprints from the other tracks. It all makes sense—Phoot is the Phantom! But why would he want to call off his own performance?'

Selby went home and crept into the study where he phoned the composer's motel.

'Sorry to wake you, Mr Phoot,' Selby said, 'but I have to talk to you.'

'It's all right, I wasn't sleeping,' the composer said.

'I know that you're the one who threw that threatening paper plane.'

'You do? Who are you? How could you possibly know?'

'I do. Never mind. And I know you ran backwards across that field,' Selby said, answering all three questions in order. 'Why did you do it?'

There was a long sigh.

'The symphony,' the composer said. 'It isn't good enough. I needed an excuse to cancel opening night.'

'But it's great,' Selby said. 'I was there at the rehearsal and everyone loved it.'

'You're a musician—a member of the BSDS?'

'No, I'm not a musician.'

'But you were at the rehearsal?'

'Yes.'

'Then you must be a dog. The only one who wasn't a musician at the rehearsal was a dog.'

'So, I'm a musician,' Selby said. 'But never mind about that. I think you should go ahead with the performance tomorrow night.'

'Why?'

'Because everyone's looking forward to it.'

'That's what I've been thinking too,' the old man said. 'Okay, I'll go ahead with it. You've convinced me. But please don't tell anyone what you know.'

'Don't worry, I won't,' Selby said.

The next night Bogusville Hall was packed as *The Great Chicken Disaster Symphony* came to its stirring conclusion. For a second everyone just sat in their seats, stunned. Then they jumped

to their feet, cheering and screaming even louder than the symphony itself.

'That was brilliant!' Mrs Trifle said after the concert as she handed the composer a bouquet of flowers from the BSDS.

'Oh, thank you so much,' Jango Phoot said. 'I'm so happy that everyone liked my new work. And I'm so glad that I came to Bogusville to perform it. It has given me confidence. I can't wait to get home and work on my new, much quieter piece: *The Running Through the Mud*

Symphony. I will dedicate it to the Phantom Phonecaller—whoever he may be.'

'Phantom Phonecaller,' Selby thought. 'That's me! A real live symphony dedicated to little old Selby! This is wonderful! And I owe it all to *The Art of the Private Investigator*. Without it I never would have known that those footprints were really Phootprints.'

UNDERGROUND UNDERDOG

'There's been a terrible accident!' Mrs Trifle said. 'It was just on the news. Gwendolyn Krater is trapped at the bottom of Gumboot Cave!'

'Not *the* Gwendolyn Krater?' Dr Trifle said.

'Yes, Barrington Krater's sister.'

'But they're the best cave explorers in the country.'

'And the most reckless, if you ask me,' Mrs Trifle said. 'Apparently Gwendolyn found another cave in the bottom of Gumboot Cave. She fell down a shaft and can't get back up.'

'Why doesn't Barrington just go down after her?'

'He's too big. Gwendolyn's tiny and she just barely fitted down the shaft. He tried dropping a rope down the shaft but it wouldn't go. The

Cave Rescue Services' drilling equipment is coming, but it won't be here till tomorrow.'

'Just thinking about it gives me that horrible feeling about being in tight places. You know, that Santa Claus thing.'

'Claustrophobia.'

'That's it.'

'Sheeeeesh! I hate caves,' Selby thought. 'Why do people want to explore them? Why can't they just stay up here in the fresh air and enjoy life?'

'There's another problem,' Mrs Trifle said. 'The water is rising in the cave and Gwendolyn could drown if she isn't rescued soon.'

'Drown? Shivers!' Selby thought. 'Stuck down a cave with the water coming up. Just thinking about it makes my heart beat like a bongo drum.'

'I have an idea,' Dr Trifle said, dashing for his workroom. 'I've got some equipment that might help. Jump in the car and let's go!'

Twenty minutes later, when the Trifles arrived at the entrance to Gumboot Cave, Barrington Krater was there with some reporters. Dr Trifle slung his rucksack over his shoulder.

'I have some sophisticated rescue equipment

here,' Dr Trifle said without bothering to say hello. 'Take us down to the new shaft and we'll see if we can rescue your sister.'

'Great!' Barrington said. 'Let's go!'

'Selby, you stay here,' Mrs Trifle said.

'Nonsense! Come along, old dog, old bean,' Barrington said, grabbing Selby's lead and pulling him into the cave. 'Dogs love caves. They don't have any of the silly fears that people do.'

'Have I got news for you,' Selby thought as Barrington pulled him into Gumboot Cave. 'Oh, woe, it's so dark and creepy in here.'

And down they went . . . and down . . . and down, lighting the cave ahead with their torches.

'It's not too bad so far,' Selby thought after a while. 'As long as the tunnels are nice and big, it's not too scary.'

The Trifles followed Barrington down a steep winding path to a huge open gallery at the bottom.

'I can never remember what those things are called,' Mrs Trifle said, pointing her torch around.

'Stalactites and stalagmites,' Barrington said matter-of-factly.

'Yes, but which is which?'

'Easy: the icicles on the ceiling are the

stalactites and the ice cream cones on the floor are *stalagmites*. Just remember that mites go up and tights come down and you'll never forget which is which.'

'Mites go up and tights come down,' said Mrs Trifle. 'Very good. But, come to think of it, can't a mite go down as well as up?'

'Yes, I suppose one could.'

'And if tights come down, don't they go up first?'

'You're right,' Barrington said. 'Now I've forgotten which is which. Oh, well.'

Barrington led the Trifles around behind a stalagmite—or maybe it was a stalactite—to a hole in the ground.

'This is it,' he said. 'She's down there.'

'But it's tiny!' Mrs Trifle exclaimed.

'It was tight even for Gwen,' Barrington said. 'She had to kind of squiggle her way into it, headfirst. Then I heard her slide down the shaft.'

'But she might be . . . she might have . . . passed on or something.'

'Gwen, dead?' Barrington said. 'No. Injured, perhaps, but I'm sure she's okay. It's just a matter of getting a line down to her.'

Selby put his head into the entrance of the

hole and listened to the sound of rushing water in the distance.

'Merciful heaven,' he thought. 'I think I'm going to faint just thinking of Gwen squiggling down this narrow shaft.'

Meanwhile, Dr Trifle had unpacked his rucksack.

'Is this your sophisticated rescue equipment?' Barrington asked. 'It looks more like a toy truck. What are we supposed to do with that?'

'Yes,' Dr Trifle admitted, 'Supa-Truk was invented as a toy, but with my newly invented Mini-Light and a Mini-Cam it should be perfect to find your sister.'

'And the string?'

'It's not string; it's ultra-thin, high-tension, fibre-optical cable,' Dr Trifle said, starting the truck wheels in motion and putting it in the hole. 'Now keep your eyes on the monitor.'

They all watched the TV monitor as Supa-Truk wound its way down the steep hole and into the shaft. There was a pinpoint of light at the bottom.

'That's her!' Barrington cried. 'I can see Gwen's torch!'

The tiny light got bigger and bigger and then,

suddenly, a jet of water shot out of the side of the tunnel and the TV picture disappeared.

'Oh, no!' Dr Trifle said. 'Short circuit. I was afraid of that. Supa-Truk isn't waterproof.'

'Just keep lowering it down. My sister will see it, clip the line to her belt, and we can pull her up.'

'How will we know when she's ready to be pulled up?' Mrs Trifle said.

'Three strong tugs,' Barrington said. 'That's the usual signal.'

'Oh, bother,' Dr Trifle said. 'The truck won't go down. It must be caught on something.'

For the next few minutes, Dr Trifle pulled Supa-Truk up and dropped it again and again.

'I'm afraid it's no use,' he said, finally pulling the truck back up and out of the hole. 'We'll just have to wait for the cave rescue equipment.'

'It'll be too late,' Barrington whimpered. 'Oh, poor Gwenny.'

For a minute everyone sat silently in the dark, their torches making eerie shadows on the ceiling.

'Now I guess she'll drown,' Selby thought. 'I feel so sorry for her—and for her brother—and for the Trifles. *Sniff.* This is so sad.'

'We need somebody small to squiggle down that shaft,' Barrington said. 'It's our only hope.'

'We can't go lowering children down to the bowels of the earth,' Mrs Trifle said. 'It's simply not allowed.'

'I don't mean a child,' Barrington said, eyeing Selby. 'What about your dog?'

Selby felt his blood run cold.

'What about me?' Selby thought. 'I wouldn't go down there for all the beetroot in Bogusville!'

'It's no good,' Mrs Trifle said. 'We couldn't do that to him.'

'Well, *I* could,' Barrington said, clipping Dr Trifle's line to Selby's collar.

'Hey! Stop!' Selby thought, as he struggled to get free.

'What will he do when he gets down there?' Dr Trifle asked.

'He doesn't have to do a thing. Gwen will clip the line to her belt, pull on the line, and then we'll pull her up.'

'How about Selby?' Dr Trifle asked.

'Yeah, how about me?' Selby thought, his knees now so weak that they wobbled.

'She could tie him to herself,' Barrington said. 'It's worth a try. I mean, we're talking about my sister's life. You can always get a new dog—I can't get a new sister.'

'Sheeeeesh!' Selby thought. 'I'd try to run away or I'd bite or something but I'm so dizzy I can't move. Somebody please stop the cave from spinning! I think I'm going to talk. Yes, that's it. I'm going to tell them that I know how to talk. I'll reason with them. I'll talk them out of sending me down there.'

But before Selby could say, 'Excuse me, but I'm the only talking dog in Australia—and perhaps the world—and there's no way I'm going down that hole,' Barrington whisked him off the ground.

'The dog is our only chance,' he cried, thrusting Selby headfirst into the hole.

Selby plummetted headlong, headfirst and headdown into the shaft with his legs stiff as steel as he went faster and faster.

'Yooooooowwwwwww! I'm going to die! I'm gone! I'm a dead dog! This is worse than kissing Aunt Jetty! It's so tight in here!' he thought. 'I just feel like clawing my way back up to fresh air! Maybe that's why they call it *claws*-trophobia. He, he, he, he.'

Selby giggled at his joke and then giggled some more

'Oh, no! Now I'm losing my mind! I can't

stop giggling! I've got to stop giggling and keep my wits about me.'

Suddenly Selby came to a slippery stop, but before he could turn around and try to scramble back up, he lost his footing again and slid down a second shaft all the way to the bottom of a big, open cavern filled with stalactites and stalagmites.

Selby was about to give three strong tugs on the line to get them to pull him back up when he saw Gwendolyn lying unconscious next to him on the ground, her torch still burning brightly.

'Uh-oh, the water's rising!' Selby said as he unclipped the line from his collar and attached it to Gwendolyn's climbing belt. He pushed her sideways and then sat her up with her head sticking up into the shaft.

'So far, so good,' Selby thought as the water suddenly came up around his ankles. 'Now all I have to do is hang onto her legs and they'll pull us both up.'

Selby pulled three times on the ultra-thin, high-tension line, but before he could get a good grip on the unconscious Gwendolyn, she shot up the shaft.

'Hey, wait for me!' Selby screamed above the sound of the rushing water. 'Oh, no! The

water's rising! I've got to get to higher ground!'

Selby scrambled onto a stalagmite—or was it a stalactite?—as the water rose around him. As it reached his feet, he took a leap upwards and grabbed a stalactite on the ceiling—or was it a stalagmite?—and began climbing it, centimetre by centimetre as the water rose. Soon he was at the very top of the cave with nowhere to go.

'This is it!' he said. 'I'm a goner!'

Just then, by the light of the floating torch, Selby noticed a crack in the roof. He put a paw into it and then another paw and the rock gave way, making it an almost-dog-size crack.

'I'll squeeze myself up into here and hope the water goes down again.'

Selby wriggled up and up into the crack with the water licking his toes. But as he went the crack got bigger and bigger and bigger and finally it opened out into another cavern. And across the way in the dim light Selby saw the shapes of the Trifles and Barrington bending over Gwendolyn.

'Where am I?' she asked. 'What's happening?'

'You're alive!' Barrington cried. 'And you're safe and sound!'

'Where's that big hairy man who helped to rescue me?'

'Big hairy man?' Barrington asked. 'I'm afraid you must have imagined him. The only one down there with you was a medium-sized hairy dog.'

'Poor Selby,' Mrs Trifle sniffed. 'Oh, my poor, poor dog. I'll never forgive you for this, Barrington. You sacrificed the most wonderful dog in the world.'

'I think I'll just stand here for a minute,' Selby thought, 'and hear what they thought about me. It isn't often you get to hear your own funeral speeches.'

'He was a truly warm and wonderful dog,' Dr Trifle said, hugging Mrs Trifle.

'There has never been a dog like Selby,' Mrs Trifle added. 'We loved him so, so much.'

'Gosh,' Selby thought as he blushed a little dog-like blush. 'They really did like me.'

'What a dog,' Dr Trifle said. 'He may not have been perfect; he wasn't the most energetic dog in the world, but we loved him.'

'Hey, now wait a minute,' Selby thought.

'You might even say that he was lazy,' Mrs Trifle said.

'And of course he could be cranky at times,' Dr Trifle added.

'He may not even have been perfect,' Mrs Trifle said, 'but—'

Suddenly, somewhere in the darkness behind them, the Trifles heard a loud bark.

HIGH HAT HARRY THE HAPPY HYPNOTIST

*in which everyone in Bogusville
finally finds out Selby's secret*

All of Bogusville was going to the town hall to see High Hat Harry the Happy Hypnotist do his Magic of the Mind Free-for-All Show.

'It's absolutely free,' Mrs Trifle said. 'It doesn't cost a cent.'

'How is that possible?' asked Dr Trifle. 'Don't we have to buy tickets?'

'No. At the end of the show, Harry passes his hat around. You can donate anything you want. If you don't enjoy yourself, you don't have to give anything.'

'He sounds like an honest man to me,' said Dr Trifle who was very careful with his money. 'Let's go tonight. It could be fun.'

'It's not fair,' Selby thought as he watched the Trifles' car drive away. 'Everybody gets to go but me. I want to see High Hat Harry too. Well, I'm going anyway. So there!'

Selby ran off down the street to the town hall. He crept in and hid behind the curtain that covered the back wall. Standing on his hind legs, he could see out over the audience. Harry was standing on stage wearing a huge hat.

'Well, here I am in Bogusville,' Harry said. 'Aren't I a lucky dog?'

Everyone laughed.

'So which one of you brave people is going to be my first victim?' Everyone laughed but no one volunteered. 'How about you, Mayor Trifle?'

Selby could see Mrs Trifle shake her head.

'Now, now, Mrs Mayor. Here's your chance to win lots of votes,' Harry said. 'Or lose them,' he said to the audience.

'Oh, all right,' Mrs Trifle said.

Everyone clapped as Mrs Trifle slowly got out of her seat and made her way to the stage.

'This won't hurt, will it?' she asked the hypnotist.

'Of course not,' Harry said. 'Now just relax and watch my hand.'

Harry moved his hand back and forth slowly and then in a circle that got smaller and smaller.

'You are getting very sleepy,' he said.

Harry's hand came closer and closer to Mrs Trifle's face. When he snapped his fingers her head suddenly tilted.

'It worked!' Selby thought. 'He actually hypnotised her. This is great!'

'You are in my power,' Harry said. 'Do you hear me?'

'I am in your power,' Mrs Trifle said very slowly.

'You are back in school,' Harry said, 'playing in the playground at recess. Do you see all the other children out there?'

'Yes, I do,' Mrs Trifle said, putting on a little girl's voice and looking at the audience.

'I think they need some cheering up, don't you?'

'Why, so they do,' Mrs Trifle said.

With this, Mrs Trifle started pulling silly faces and making rude noises by putting her tongue between her lips and blowing. Everyone roared with laughter.

'That certainly cheered them up,' Harry cried, clapping along with everyone else. 'Now when I count to three and snap my fingers, you will wake up and you will forget everything you just did, okay? One, two, three.'

Snap!

Selby heard the snap of Harry's fingers and suddenly Mrs Trifle woke up.

'What did you want me to do?' she asked.

'You've already done it,' Harry answered. 'You were so good that I'm sure you'll be re-elected.'

Everyone laughed and cheered as the puzzled Mrs Trifle went back to her seat. Selby pulled the curtains farther apart and saw Dr Trifle whispering in Mrs Trifle's ear.

'Isn't High Hat Harry great?!' Selby squealed. 'I'd love to know how to hypnotise people.'

Next Madame Mascara came up and soon she, too, was hypnotised. She did cartwheels across the stage cackling like a hen. After her, Postie Paterson recited a rhyme about his second grade teacher, Mrs Tidley, that went:

> *Mrs Tidley had a cold*
> *And blew a bubble out her nose*
> *When she saw what she had done*

She blew another just for fun.

Postie Paterson did a little curtsy as everyone screamed with laughter.

'I beg your pardon!' a voice cried out.

Everyone laughed again as they turned to see old Mrs Tidley herself, standing in the audience with her hands on her hips. After a second she, too, burst out laughing.

'It's a good thing she has a sense of humour,' Selby thought.

Postie Paterson went back to his seat and asked the people next to him what he'd done.

For the next half hour, High Hat Harry had the most unlikely people playing hopscotch and wiggling around the floor like worms. He even had Sergeant Short of the Bogusville police singing, 'I'm a little teapot, short and stout'.

Finally the hypnotist sent everyone off the stage.

'Now I'd like you all to watch my hand,' Harry said, moving it in a slow circle. 'Everyone watching please. Slowly, slowly. You are getting very sleepy.'

'He's going to hypnotise the whole audience,' Selby thought. 'How exciting!'

In a minute, Harry had everyone mooing like a hundred cows and scratching around in their seats like chickens.

'He's done it! This is great!' Selby said, letting out a couple of moos and scratching the carpet with his feet. 'This is *soooo* weird!'

'All right, all right,' Harry said, finally. 'That brings us to the end of the show. Did you all have a good time?'

'Yes!' everyone shouted.

'Then you may wish to help a poor hypnotist pay his rent,' Harry said, taking off his huge hat, 'by making a small donation.'

Harry handed his hat to someone in the front row who got out his wallet and took out a five dollar note.

'Only five dollars?' Harry laughed. 'Is that all I'm worth? How about the rest?'

The man laughed and then reached into his wallet and took out all his money and put it in the hat.

'That's more like it,' Harry said.

Selby watched with delight as people took out their handbags and wallets and put all their money in the hat. Even Dr and Mrs Trifle put all their money in. Soon the hat came back to Harry, overflowing with money.

'If he had sold tickets, he never would have made this much money,' Selby thought. 'This High Hat Harry certainly is a clever guy.'

'Did I miss anyone?' Harry asked.

'You missed me!'

The voice came from the back of the hall. Suddenly the curtain parted and there was Selby. There was a gasp from the crowd.

'I beg your pardon?' Harry said, squinting towards Selby.

Selby felt a warm glow of happiness as he raced up to the stage.

'I said that you missed me,' Selby laughed. 'But it won't do you a bit of good because I don't carry a wallet!'

'Crikey!' Harry blurted out. 'A t-t-t-talking dog!'

'Selby!' Mrs Trifle called out. 'You can talk?'

'Perfectly,' Selby said proudly.

'But you never told us,' Dr Trifle said.

'Well, now you know,' Selby laughed. 'And it's all because of you, Harry. You did me a big favour. I'd like to shake your hand.'

Selby stood on his hind legs and put his paw out. High Hat Harry reached for it automatically and then pulled his hand back in horror. And as he did so, Selby heard the slight snapping sound of the man's fingers accidentally rubbing together.

Suddenly Selby came to his senses.

'Oh my god, I was hypnotised!' Selby thought. 'Harry had me hypnotised and I didn't know it! He made me give away my secret! Oh, no! I'll never get out of this one! I'm a done dog! Why did I ever come here?'

'This is all your fault! You've ruined my life!' Selby yelled at Harry. A tear formed in Selby's eye and then rolled down his face, disappearing into his fur.

'One minute he's happy and the next minute he's angry. What is it with this pooch?' Harry said.

For a moment, all Selby could think of were the wonderful times he'd had living with the Trifles and the great adventures he'd had as he struggled to keep his secret a secret. Now it was over. Soon he'd be famous. People from all over would come by the busload to see the world's greatest freak of nature—an actual, real live, talking dog.

More tears formed in Selby's eyes and through them he saw the blurry shape of the man who had destroyed him—High Hat Harry. Suddenly his sadness turned to rage.

'Get out of my sight before I tear your leg off!' Selby screamed.

One sight of Selby's teeth and Harry shot out the door. In a second his car started and drove off down the road.

Selby suddenly noticed the hatful of money. He handed it to someone in the front row.

'Take back your money, everyone,' Selby said.

The hat was passed around and everyone took out what they'd put in.

'Please tell us how did you learn to talk?' Mrs Trifle said finally.

'I might as well tell you everything,' Selby said with a sigh. 'It happened a few years ago when I was watching TV. Suddenly I could understand everything everyone was saying. Then I practised and practised till I could talk.'

'You must have been so surprised to just understand like that,' Dr Trifle said.

'You can say that again,' Selby said.

'You must have been so surprised to just understand like that,' Dr Trifle said again.

Selby laughed a little Selby laugh in spite of himself.

'No, I didn't mean for you to say it again,' he said. 'It's just an expression.' Dr Trifle stared at him blankly. 'It's just like saying, "Shake a leg," when you want someone to hurry up,' Selby added.

Just then, everyone stood up and started shaking their legs.

'That's just an expression too,' Selby said. 'What's wrong with you people? It's like saying, "Well blow me down," when you're surprised.'

Suddenly everyone started blowing all at once

and a gust of wind hit Selby that nearly blew him down.

'Stop!' Selby yelled. 'You're being silly! I'm trying to be serious here!'

'Crumbs!' Selby thought. 'They're all hypnotised! No wonder they gave all of their money! Harry *told* them to. He was robbing them! They're still hypnotised because they didn't hear Harry's fingers snap. I think I've just been saved!'

'All right, everyone,' Selby announced. 'The show is over. Now, when I count to three, you're going to wake up. You'll forget everything—especially the bit about me talking, okay? One, two, three,' Selby said. 'Uh-oh, I can't snap my fingers. I don't *have* any fingers! What am I going to do? The whole of Bogusville could be hypnotised forever! Now wait a minute. Could you all please snap your fingers?'

There was an almighty clatter of snapping and everyone suddenly woke up.

'I guess the show's over,' someone said. 'But where's High Hat Harry?'

'Well, Harry said he was a lucky dog to be in Bogusville,' someone else yelled, pointing at

Selby, 'and now I guess he's turned into one.'

Everyone roared with laughter as Selby raced from the stage and headed for home.

'Lucky dog is right,' Selby thought. 'Now I'm the *luckiest* dog in Australia—and perhaps the world!'

Song for a Dog Detective
(the hard version)

Music by Kathryn Lambert

Song for a Dog Detective
(the easy version)

Words by Selby.

Music by Kathryn Lambert

Don't cry and don't wail, There's a dog on your tail. You've noth-ing to fear, If you're in the clear, But if you're a crook, Then have a good look. If you're a crim then you'll know that it's him!

CHORUS

Sel - by sup-er-snoop Sel - by sup-er-snoop He's a sup-er-dup-er snoop Poo-poo-pi-doop Sel-by!

Verse 2:

A sight to be seen,
With hearing so keen,
He really can't fail,
This dog on your tail.

The baddies say 'Crumbs,
Look out! Here he comes!',
Up to the end,
He's a goodie's best friend.

Chorus:
Selby supersnoop,
Selby supersnoop,
He's a super-duper snoop,
Poo poo pi doop.

Verse 3:

When you're in the poo,
This dog will come through,
So don't shed a tear,
For Selby is here.

No problem will strain,
His mega-size brain,
So give a shout,
'Cos the secret is out.

Chorus:
Selby supersnoop,
Selby supersnoop,
He's a super-duper snoop,
Poo poo pi doop.

AFTERWORD

I certainly had some close calls, didn't I? Phew! I don't know how much longer I can keep my secret a secret. I only wish I had lots and lots of money and then I could tell the Trifles my secret and it wouldn't matter if they knew. If anyone wanted me to do some work or something, I could always pay someone else to do it.

But I can't complain. The Trifles are wonderful to me and I have a very happy life (most of the time). And being happy is what really matters isn't it?

Your happy friend,

Selby